One Day's
Perfect Weather

OTHER BOOKS BY DANIEL STERN

The Girl with the Glass Heart
The Guests of Fame
Miss America
Who Shall Live, Who Shall Die
The Suicide Academy
The Rose Rabbi
After the War
Final Cut
An Urban Affair
Twice Told Tales
Twice Upon a Time

One Day's Perfect Weather

More Twice Told Tales

DANIEL STERN

SOUTHERN METHODIST
UNIVERSITY PRESS
Dallas

These stories are works of fiction. Names, characters, places, and incidents are either the product of the author's imagination or are used fictitiously.

Requests for permission to reproduce material from this work should be sent to:
Rights and Permissions
Southern Methodist University Press
PO Box 750415
Dallas, Texas 75275-0415

Copyright acknowledgments appear on page 204.

Jacket and text design: Tom Dawson

Library of Congress Cataloging-in-Publication Data

Stern, Daniel, 1928–
  One day's perfect weather : more twice told tales / Daniel Stern.
  — 1st ed.
    p.   cm.
ISBN 0-87074-445-3 (acid-free paper)
    1. United States—Social life and customs—20th century Fiction.
I. Title.
PS3569.T3887054   1999
813'.54—dc21   99-36813

Printed in the United States of America on acid-free paper

10   9   8   7   6   5   4   3   2   1

In memory of Bernard Malamud,
with love and deepest admiration.

Happiness Makes Up in Height for What It Lacks in Length

by Robert Frost

Oh, stormy, stormy world,
The days you were not swirled
Around with mist and cloud,
Or wrapped as in a shroud,
And the sun's brilliant ball
Was not in part or all
Obscured from mortal view—
Were days so very few
I can but wonder whence
I get the lasting sense
Of so much warmth and light.
If my mistrust is right
It may be altogether
From one day's perfect weather,
When starting clear at dawn,
The day swept clearly on
To finish clear at eve.
I verily believe
My fair impression may
Be all from that one day
No shadow crossed but ours
As through its blazing flowers
We went from house to wood
For change of solitude.

Contents

Author's Note

ABOUT TEN YEARS (and three books) ago I began a fresh literary adventure. I had come to a stage in my writing and personal life in which the life of literature seemed to offer an array of subjects as vast as the life of work and love, wives, children, lovers, colleagues, strangers—otherwise known as life. I wrote at one point that "a text by a writer of the past whom I loved, even a nonfiction work, could be basic to a fiction; as basic as a love affair, a trauma, a house, a mother, a landscape, a lover, a job, or a sexual passion."

I called these books (with an immodest bow to Nathaniel Hawthorne) Twice Told Tales. They are my attempt to build a strong bridge between literature and life. Such bridges have certainly been built by other writers. Among my favorite bridge-builders are Jorge Luis Borges and Nathaniel Hawthorne, to whom I've paid homage in a story, previously published, called "Wakefield by Nathaniel Hawthorne," which is told through the eyes of an essay by Borges. Two at a blow.

I believe that, with or without knowing it, regardless of the level of our education or our reading, all of us carry within us, in more or less complex degree, the basic thrust of Kafka, Melville, Robert Frost, Freud, and all the other great authors who have become the very intellectual and spiritual air we breathe. What I set out to do was to make stories that would have their own narrative life but still reflect the inspiring passions and concepts of these writers. Sexual passion, music, death, love, hate, nostalgia, art, divorce, youth: all these are obviously the stuff of life, but also of literature. It has been my happy task to try to merge them.

In this way, in earlier books, I was able to allow an idea of Freud's to inform a comedy of the bringing up of a child in a restaurant, to allow a black student in Brooklyn to embody the goals and passions of one of Henry James's super-attenuated butlers, to allow a disenchanted movie producer to live out his obsession with Hemingway's little story "A Clean, Well-Lighted Place."

In *One Day's Perfect Weather* I have essayed seven new adventures. For which I am deeply indebted to the great authors who have (all unwittingly) joined me.

DANIEL STERN
Houston
June 1999

The Taste of Pennies

Inspired by "The Oven Bird,"
a poem by Robert Frost

It was the long bad time after the long good time.

Stocks a puzzle, real estate stalled, the bond market iffy, Wall Street firms down to half their size. Two of his former associates under indictment: Sorkin and Menninger, Menninger probably guilty. To Lee Binstock, good times had always come like sunshine on a holiday weekend; a feeling of surprise but of pleasure deserved. Now that the bad times had come, he was out of work for the first time in twenty years, and he felt the unpleasant surprise of being caught and punished in spite of feeling innocent. And, of course, there was the matter of Binstock's mouth.

Always, he'd been able to make his own extracurricular comfort; the clarinet's woody breath of independence—his horn of romance. He had partners in crime. Callahan, advertising copy, ruddy, volatile, on the violin, with his quiet academic wife, second fiddle in more ways than one; Menninger, mutual funds, intense, humorless, on viola; Sorkin, arbitrage, smooth but folksy, controlling the pulse on cello. No "civilian," as they called those who could only listen, could know what a Sunday afternoon spent summoning the Brahms Quintet could do; a single-minded song to ransom the frustrations of buying too much and selling too little, to pardon the mistakes of the week, the wrong choices of a lifetime.

You can see why, once it was clear that he could not make a clean, steady sound on the clarinet anymore, might never again, Binstock was thrown into despair. He had actually—at rock bottom one night—called a Suicide Hot Line advertised in the *Village Voice*. The woman on the phone had answered, "Suicide Hot Line—please hold." And then clicked him off onto recorded music for waiting. By the time seven minutes had gone by, the idea of being put on hold to wait for a suicide counselor seemed so absurd that his mood began to clear. Also, the music they played was a Marcello Oboe Concerto, sublimely lyric even on the phone, and he made plans to buy the recording as soon as he could get to Tower Records—which he supposed was the same as saying he'd decided to live and had not been really serious about dying.

Nevertheless, the misery returned the next day, apparently to stay. Binstock supposed he should be grateful that he never had to play for a living. But it didn't help when Eugenia suggested he try to switch over to the piano, since after the bloody fight the clarinet seemed to be finished for him.

"It's nothing you did, Lee," she said. "Don't forget that. Those guys in the car—they did something to you."

"I could have kept my mouth shut," Binstock said. "I might not have a job but at least I'd still have a mouth."

She kissed him quickly on that cue. His lips were askew since the surgery—hence the difficulty in forming a proper embouchure and getting a clean sound out of the clarinet—but he could still taste a kiss. It tasted cool and sweet—a hint of some cherrylike lipstick flavor.

"Where the hell do you think you're going?"

"Move your ass. I've got the light."

"And I've got the right of way."

"Hey, we got a walking lawyer here. Right of way . . . "

"I just meant that you're such a good musician you shouldn't waste it. It's always been more than a hobby to you. You were never just a businessman."

"Disgusting word."

"Which? Musician, businessman—?"

"Hobby. What a word to use about music."

"I knew you'd say that."

"We've been married too long. You know everything I'm going to say—"

"Married talk is like music. Just because you know how a Mozart sonata goes doesn't mean it's not going to surprise you every now and then."

"Don't be clever and charming. I'm in pain."

"Mouth pain or life pain?"

"Same thing."

"Think about trying the piano. We'll always keep body and soul together. But you have to care for your soul. LA didn't help with either."

WHEN THE MARKET HAD collapsed, when the open possibilities of the last few years all seemed to turn into dead ends, Binstock had taken them to California. Eugenia, New York to her bones as only an out-of-towner can be—Connecticut-born—objected to the choice of LA. But Binstock was in need of hope and hid behind a joke—somebody's remark that Hollywood was the only place in the world where you could die from encouragement. That was the one commodity he needed, he told her, after most of the other commodities in his world had failed him. They escaped to the Beverly Hills branch of Dean Witter, in search of hope, of encouragement.

Eugenia could do her work on either coast. She ran a newsletter for educators from home; wrote, edited, mailed—the works. "I'm pre–Industrial Revolution," went her running joke. "The last cottage industry." This made for laughter at parties but said nothing about younger ambitions, about newspaper jobs not landed, about magazines not created. The newsletter won journalism awards. It gave a modest income and it could be moved with the luggage. They waited a few weeks because the gynecologist thought Eugenia might be pregnant, but it was another false alarm.

In Los Angeles they economized: one car for the two of them. On weekends, Eugenia out playing women's doubles, Binstock took a small aristocratic pleasure in noting how cars slowed down for you when you walked across Santa Monica Boulevard, a rare West Coast bird, a pedestrian. Even so, Los Angeles gave little comfort, less encouragement. They were back in New York in seven months.

"If you're such a tough guy get out of the car."

"Just move, buster. I get out of this car you're going to be damned sorry . . . "

Then the comedy of errors on upper Broadway, a car pressing him to move as he crossed Eighty-sixth Street, an angry Binstock deciding to move at his own pace, even not to move at all—then the fistfight—the only such encounter in Binstock's adult years—crunched bone, spitting, choking on blood filling his mouth with the taste of pennies, Binstock dizzy on his knees, the police siren singing in his ears.

"Son of a bitch didn't even stick around. Broke my mouth and beat it."

That was what he'd tried to say but it didn't come out clear enough for the cops or Eugenia to understand. He said it to her, carefully, after the operation.

"Blame it on LA," Eugenia said. "The cars there slow down

when they're a mile away from a pedestrian. You got used to that. You forgot how they drive in New York."

Binstock murmured, stiff-mouthed, "I was born a pedestrian. When this bastard started to push me with his damned BMW I just got pissed off. I was too tired of being pushed."

"Because he was pushing you—or because it was a BMW?" They'd sold theirs the year after the big slowdown when they sold the house in East Hampton. They were city mice, again; reacquainted with the IRT, the Crosstown bus.

BACK FROM THE HOSPITAL, too weak to look for the next job, he looked over the mail one day, sitting on the bed, only to find a disturbing letter from Sorkin. It was a rambling note full of regrets: "I guess I did wrong things but, in some strange way, not bad things. I don't know . . . I should have known better . . . don't care about myself . . . ashamed to face Ruthie and David—I read a poem the other day, 'The Oven Bird' by Carl Sandburg. You should read it—we should all read it . . . "

These days, postoperation, Binstock was exhausted by midday and it was two P.M. He fell asleep lying on top of the covers, right where he was. The instant his eyes were closed he thought—the letter from Sorkin sounded like a suicide note. He'd never seen one but the notion troubled him. He would call as soon as he woke up to see how the poor bastard was doing. But it was the phone call from Sorkin's son, David, that woke him an hour later.

THE FUNERAL SERVICE WAS mercifully brief, though Riverside Chapel was crowded. The rabbi made no mention of suicide, speaking only, a little tactlessly Binstock thought, of temptations and sin. Binstock did not linger. The letter in his pocket was on fire—and the only way to put it out was to find out what Sorkin had meant about the Sandburg poem. You couldn't put off acting on instructions from the grave. Look what had happened to Hamlet. The trouble was, Binstock had a pretty decent library, but Sandburg was not a writer he'd ever cared enough about to keep. So the poem would have to be searched out.

Before he could find a bookstore he actually passed a public library. There was something about a public library in the middle of the afternoon that mingled convalescence with the flavor of childhood. The library was half empty, but he remembered the libraries of the past exactly that way. The computer showed all of Sandburg but there was nothing called "The Oven Bird."

Binstock found it hard to believe that Sorkin, hard-nosed, sharp-edged Sorkin, had actually read poetry. The one person in their group who busied herself with poetry readings down-town, maybe even wrote a few poems, had fallen out of touch as soon as the going got rough: Jenny Maslow. It was worth a shot, a quarter from a phone booth on the corner.

"LEE, I'M OVER HERE."

The bar in the Carlyle was blindingly dark after the cold autumn sunlight and Binstock blinked and blinked until he saw her. He said, "I can't believe I called you out of the blue and there you were."

It's hard to know who was more nervous, Binstock or this slender, almost anorectic-looking young woman—younger than he remembered.

"It just means that now I'm one of those people at home during the day. But calling about a poem! Who's going to believe that?"

When he told her about Sorkin's letter she believed it. "The tough ones melt down the quickest. I read the obit this morning, but I couldn't get myself to go."

The drinks came, a Coke for him and the real thing, something with tequila, for Jenny. "Not settled anywhere yet?" he asked.

"Ah, well," she said. "I had a good long ride. I put some away and I'm back to school. Are you still having those wonderful chamber music evenings of yours? The Mozart Quintet . . . "

It was the time to tell her about the fight and the operation and to show her his mouth a little more closely. He was grateful now that bars in the afternoon were dark.

She braved it out. "I haven't been this close to your mouth in years. Kind of nice."

Jenny had happened just before he'd met Eugenia, and Binstock had been the one to break it off. That's why he'd been too embarrassed to just ask her for information about a poem on the phone, why he'd suggested a drink when it was much too early for a drink and much too late for Jenny. When it was clear he was not picking up on her auld lang syne she said, "I'm sorry those bastards hurt you and I'm sorry about the clarinet. I know how much you loved playing. I found out in high school that I loved poetry—but I can't write worth a damn. At least you can play."

"Could," he said. "You probably know this poem Sorkin wanted me to read."

She giggled, a nervous tic more than laughter. "The answer from the grave?"

"Or a warning."

"Sorkin was wrong. 'The Oven Bird' isn't Sandburg. Can you imagine your cold-blooded partner turning away from his computer running the price of gold in Tokyo, and reading a poem to try to understand his life? He even got the poet wrong. It's by Robert Frost. My God! I mean, I'm sorry about what happened but Jesus—Sorkin, of all people."

"No soul?"

"Whatever passes for that these days—yeah, that's what I meant. But it's not Sandburg." She laughed. "This bird is way beyond old Carl Sandburg—Chicago, Hog Butcher to the world, et cetera. You know, Frost is really a dark poet—and God knows 'The Oven Bird' is one of the darker ones."

"Let's hear it." Binstock sipped his Coke carefully. He was using his mouth very carefully these days.

"Oh, I don't know it by heart." She raised her glass. A few seconds' wait and she said, "I live around the corner on Eighty-fourth Street."

"I know," Binstock said.

"Come on back and I'll dig it out and you can read it yourself."

SHE READ QUITE BEAUTIFULLY, a low husky voice without sentimental cadences, just right for this strange little item. He sipped a vodka—it was now late enough for a drink—and listened. It was not easy to get, for most of the way, a small poem, a sonnet, Jenny said it was, surprising him—Binstock didn't think people wrote sonnets after Shakespeare. It began:

> There is a singer everyone has heard,
> Loud, a mid-summer and a mid-wood bird.

It was not difficult, just hard to focus on—what the hell could Sorkin have had in mind? Then, with the last two lines, it was painful, it was clear.

> The question that he frames in all but words
> Is what to make of a diminished thing.

Jenny put the book down. "Poor bastard," she said.

"I liked him," Binstock said. "But I never quite trusted him. What kind of a man goes into arbitrage? After playing the viola in high school. Buying and selling money. Weird."

"You sound like Ezra Pound."

"What do you mean?"

"It doesn't matter," Jenny said. "Look at these lines—this was his mood when he—" She read:

> The bird would cease and be as other birds
> But that he knows in singing not to sing.
> The question that he frames in all but words . . .

Binstock murmured the last line: " 'Is what to make of a diminished thing.' Jesus, you know I could have done without this. Some favor from old Sorkin."

Jenny started to stand but instead leaned over him, the book in her hand. "I remember when I first read it. It makes your insides jump. Each time. It's always a shock. The question is when you read it. At what point. Sometimes you find those lines when you're ready for them. Other times they jump at you—a sad surprise."

"I guess Sorkin was looking for answers—and he found this."

"Found another question."

She traced his wounded mouth with a temporary caress. The kiss surprised them both. Not knowing what to do when their mouths separated she dropped the book into his hands. "Here," she said. "Take it. You can return it when you're done."

Binstock was torn—borrowed books had to be returned—usually in person. Her finger touched the scar above his lip.

"Is this where . . . ?"

Binstock stood up. What he didn't want was a mercy-fuck. Nor anything from Jenny, he realized, except the poem. Anyway, now it was his as much as hers—a dubious acquisition.

● ● ●

BACK AT HIS APARTMENT, Eugenia was still out—the books on the
shelves were waiting. But by this time Binstock was in a fuming
rage. What was this shit about a poem that Sorkin was trying to
pull on him? Was he implying that the two of them had been in
the same boat, the same bag, the same scam, choose any
crummy metaphor you want, he thought, running his fingers
along the spines of books. He'd been such an idiot that between
Sorkin and Menninger, he'd always assumed that maybe it was
Menninger who deserved the indictment—had done something tricky, just beyond the law in some gray area of right and
wrong.

Menninger had such a smooth style, while Sorkin was all sin-
cerity. Mister Straight in his collection of tattersall vests, the
country boy come to Wall Street who just got lucky—then
luckier—then, very quickly, out of luck—finished. Was this
poem by another country boy written in some code Binstock
was supposed to break, a code that would reveal the truth of
what had happened to all of them—and all the others who'd
been laid low after riding so high?

The problem was: Binstock didn't feel he belonged with the
others. He'd been like the child at the grownups' party, only half
understanding what they were talking about when their lunch
deals got cryptic, mysterious. Maybe a broker who played the
serious musician on weekends was not to be trusted with secrets
full of dirt and danger. In which case his clarinet may have saved
his ass. Who knows what he would have done given the opportunity. In any case, he wasn't knocking himself off. For Christ's
sake, he wasn't forty yet—why should he read a fucking poem
about diminished things?

Binstock pulled the book out so violently that a batch of
neighboring books tumbled to the floor. Then, without under-

standing what he was doing, he grabbed the blue-covered Frost book and tried to tear it in half. He'd never imagined what it might feel like to try to rip up a hard cover book, but he was sure it would be easy. It wasn't. The top part detached from the spine, pages ripped and dangling, but the whole thing stopped around halfway. His right hand hurt like hell and he felt like an idiot. He stood there, wondering how he would explain this scene if Eugenia walked in at that moment.

The ragged Frost was on the floor next to his foot as he kneeled trying to pick up the books in time but of course Eugenia arrived in the middle of it all.

"What's going on?"

"I don't know," Binstock said.

She zeroed in on the ripped-up Frost before he had a chance to hide it.

"My God, what is this?" She picked it up. It dangled from her hand, a wounded bird, survivor of some terrible accident.

"I'm sorry."

"It's not even yours. It belonged to Richard."

"I didn't think of that."

"Maybe you did. Are you still weird about him?"

Richard was Eugenia's first husband, an architect, first divorced, now dead in a plane crash three years ago.

"I was never weird about Richard."

"You acted like a crazy person whenever I mentioned him."

"Maybe you did that a little too often."

"Oh, for God's sake, Lee."

"Anyway, this is about Sorkin, my ex-partner, not your ex-husband."

She pushed her coat off her shoulders and let it fall among the books.

"I forgot about him mentioning some poem. Is this it? I thought it was Sandburg."

"It was Frost. Sorkin didn't know anything about poetry. Neither do I. But I don't go around writing letters scaring people—and then dying—not just dying—killing myself."

"Did that scare you?"

"Well, it freaked me."

She walked the torn and flapping book into the living room. Binstock did not follow her. He knelt among the books and started replacing them on the shelves. Then he hung up Eugenia's coat. When he was finished he went into the living room. He lay down on the couch and picked up yesterday's *Wall Street Journal*, half scanning it, half hiding behind it.

She was quiet a long time. He heard her exhale, a long, slow breath.

Binstock has been hoping she would get to the lines in question—and just read them, in some cool and detached grown-up Eugenia way. Instead she seems taken out of herself.

"Diminished thing . . . ," she breathes. "How did he know?"

Binstock puts down the paper. Eugenia is leaning back, her finger marking the last two lines of the poem. He asks her what she means—how did he know what? She tells him she'd always counted herself as reasonably happy, lucky, but if you think about diminished things, how could she not count up all the times, the lessening, the shrinking, the losing . . . ? "My God," she murmurs.

"What do you mean, exactly?" he asks, all innocence. "Be specific."

"It's not just now—early middle or whatever I'm in. It's every time—when I was fourteen I thought I would never again feel the heights of the year before when these two seniors, Larry and Bart, competed for me—and I ignored them both and wrote an essay on independence for a school contest, instead, that got published in the *Atlantic Monthly*, special teenager's section. And do you remember, when you first met me, how

I played tennis with a natural backhand motion out of Balanchine? Now, I have to think carefully, 'Get the racket back, bend your knees' . . . Diminished things . . ." She gently folds the torn book closed.

It was a strange moment—she'd taken the whole question from him and made it her own; had gone from surprised anger to introspection so quickly. All it took was a few lines of a poem. At the same time, she took the idea of diminishment so lightly; just a minor joke played on us all; took the Oven Bird's song down to questions of a fourteen-year-old's essay . . . of a tennis backhand.

"Let's eat out tonight," he said.

"I have veal defrosting."

Eugenia had been cooking home every night for months, avoiding the hefty restaurant checks of the good old days.

"If I'm tearing up books you can melt some veal."

She left the Frost on the couch, torn and helpless, open to the Oven Bird's page.

THEY PICKED AN ITALIAN place which was on a special discount card: 20 percent off everything, tax and tip included. Binstock ordered a double vodka Gibson, surprising both of them.

"A double?" Eugenia used her eyebrows.

"Not to worry. Twenty percent off."

They both knew she hadn't meant the money but she let it pass.

"Did Richard really like poetry a lot?"

"Are we back to Richard?"

Eugenia ordered a glass of the house red while Binstock worked a little too swiftly on his double vodka. It was not Elio's, it was not Primola, it was certainly not 21—though the tables had white tablecloths, not checkered cloth or paper—they weren't down to that yet. But there was little likelihood of running into anybody they knew. They were between lives. Old friends still ate and summered in places they would not now be able to afford. New friends are not made so easily after thirty-five. Once, at two in the morning, Eugenia had wakened and murmured to him something about depending too much on each other. Binstock had said, "Who's to say what's too much?" and turned back to sleep.

"Actually," she said, "Richard was more visual. He liked some poetry but nothing too complicated. And God knows he wasn't the kind who would try to find some truth about himself from a poem. Have we now maybe had enough about Richard and have you maybe had enough vodka?"

His hand had been in the air to catch the waiter's eye while she was talking. But by this time the waiter was there and he was ordering another double Gibson and Eugenia was carefully reading her way through the pastas. When he'd gotten irritated enough at her silent menu-reading act, Binstock tossed back about half of his second drink in one gulp; a dramatic toss, the way he'd seen actors do it in the movies.

But the drama backfired. The vodka went down the wrong way and he couldn't bring up a breath. Eugenia heard the awful wheeze and screech of his trying to breathe and she stood up.

"Lee, are you all right?"

Binstock couldn't answer, just kept trying to pull air up, desperately hoping that the block would give. He felt an instant away from being able to breathe again and at the same time an instant away from dying. He was terrified. It went on longer than he could have believed. He didn't think you could do without air for that long. People at the next table stared. The waiter appeared.

"Are you all right, sir?" The only question in the world anybody seemed to be able to ask at such a moment: "Are you all right?"

Eugenia came behind him and grabbed him, pulling up from his chair. She put her arms around his chest in some amateur's version of the rescue techniques they'd seen demonstrated on television. Then she squeezed hard. Binstock didn't want her to do that. He screeched even worse but felt a bit of air get through. Then, suddenly, it was over. He could get a half-breath in, and finally a sort of regular flow of air began.

All he could say was, "I'm sorry, I'm sorry . . ."

BINSTOCK HAD NEVER DRUNK so much so quickly and Eugenia had to put him to bed. But the alcohol made him edgy, alert even as it wore off. When Eugenia went to the kitchen to make coffee he sneaked into the bathroom and took a Valium—sneaked it because they both knew you didn't mix Valium and liquor. But when she came back with the coffee he told her and she just laughed and poured the coffee. "It's been that kind of day," she said. "Tearing up books, vodka, Valium, almost choking to death. Not necessarily in that order."

Sipping, sitting up, he said, "Maybe I was still competing with Sorkin."

"I don't think choking to death is highly recommended for suicide. Too painful, too unsure."

"It felt pretty close to dying—it feels that way when you can't breathe for so long."

"We keep talking about taking a course in CPR."

He put the empty cup down on the tray and lay back. "I feel like Lazarus back from the dead."

"How does it feel?"

"Strange. More peaceful than I've been for days, maybe weeks or months."

Eugenia picked up the tray to take it back to the kitchen. Binstock saw that her hands were trembling. He let her go without saying anything; he felt tranquil—too quick for the Valium—as if he'd come out on the other side of something. She came back to see him off to sleep and he was too sleepy now to notice if her hands were still shaky.

"Are you all right, Lee?"

"Yes. I'll get another job, a good one. Not to worry."

"You scared me to death when you couldn't breathe."

"Almost."

"Well, almost to death."

"I felt pretty close myself. No air, God . . ."

Eugenia tightened the sheets, smoothed the blankets with quick, nervous movements and sat down on the bed.

"Will you be able to sleep?"

He was almost asleep already, he told her, and after all he still had a mouth—to smile with, to kiss with, to eat with—maybe a little more cautiously than before. Had he told her, he asked, with the odd solemnity of receding drunkenness, that he'd spent his childhood waiting in asthma clinics with his mother— that he'd desperately wanted to play the violin but they'd given him the clarinet, instead, because the doctor thought it would be good for his poor constricted, twitchy lungs?

"No," she said. "Did it work?"

"Yes. It worked, a lot of things work until they don't anymore."

Eugenia folded blankets around him and said, "It's just an idea to you—a poem—but I've seen oven birds—they're a kind of warbler—like a thrush. We had lots of them at the farm in Haddam before my grandfather sold it. A brown back with white across the breast. It has a funny cry—it goes 'TeacherteacherteacherteacherTEACHER' getting louder and louder—then it stops."

"Country girl," he murmured. "If it's a teacher we can ask it what all this means, what's happened to us."

"Maybe it doesn't know, maybe it's only calling for its teacher. And besides, it's a bird that doesn't answer questions—only asks—and only asks one question, according to the poem . . . What to make of—"

"Yes."

He murmured, "I wonder did Sorkin's suicide note do this to us, tonight, or was it Mister Frost's bird?" He began to drift off even though he wanted to stay and be of some comfort to her as she had been to him, but he was too far gone. The risk of danger from mixing vodka and Valium was apparently avoided—but not the drowsiness.

Drifting into sleep Binstock thinks about his mother, standing in line at the clinic, holding the card with the visits checked off, her calm manner hiding the nervous chain smoker, the courageous woman afraid of everything, supervising his pre-scribed home exercises: breathe in deeply, breathe out even more deeply, empty your lungs—push. His mother who'd always made do with so little, asked even less, but had been granted at least the largesse of height—a statuesque, lofty carriage. And Bin-stock remembers how even that had diminished at the last, and she cast a short, sickly shadow on the way out.

BINSTOCK WAKES IN A sudden state of joy. It is almost morning going by the light seeping at the corners of the shutters. His mouth is dry and his head hurts but he has the answer. With the foolish clarity of dreams it presents itself as a sublimely simple solution: sell the clarinet. He knows it is irrational, that it solves nothing, but somehow removing the physical presence of the clarinet, as a reminder of loss, of what could no longer be per-formed, at least not decently, feels like a freedom. Once it is out of the house Binstock can start again—find new opportunities, new consolations. He wonders how much you could get for a used Buffet B-flat clarinet, in good condition. Quietly, Binstock steps out of bed, past his sleeping wife, out of the bedroom.

He unhooks the case and holds up the instrument. The silver keys glimmer in a strobe of light as he turns it in his hands, the black wood gleaming the only way wood knows how to gleam when competing with silver, but lovely in its own dark ways. If he kept it, it would not be like other clarinets, would never again sing the Brahms or the Mozart . . .

He hears the echo of the lines and goes into the living room where the ripped Frost book is still lying on the couch. He finds:

> The bird would cease and be as other birds
> But that he knows in singing not to sing.

His eyes roam the page looking for other lines that had pissed him off in yesterday's state of rage—confusing him but not consoling. It is different this morning. In the kitchen, holding the book, Binstock pours himself a glass of orange juice, comes back to the couch and reads the fourteen lines. Then he gets a white lined pad from his desk, takes out the Mont Blanc fountain pen Eugenia had bought him when they'd first made him a vice-president at Merrill Lynch. He begins to copy out the sonnet. It is comforting to roll out the words; he understands why people in mourning go back to school so often.

Binstock thinks—this is not such a big deal. It's as if he'd spent his life reading and understanding poems.

> There is a singer everyone has heard,
> Loud, a mid-summer and a mid-wood bird,
> Who makes the solid tree trunks sound again.

A pause to reread. Midsummer is what counts here, he thinks. For this miserable bird, midsummer is already too late, the peak is over. God! what a pain.

> He says that leaves are old and that for flowers
> Mid-summer is to spring as one to ten.

Midsummer is practically the end of everything, compared to spring. And old leaves—a mysterious phrase: how old can leaves be? Every year they must age about the same before they fall . . .

> He says the early petal-fall is past
> When pear and cherry bloom went down in showers
> On sunny days a moment overcast;

Everything good seems to be past—which rhymes with overcast . . . downer after downer . . .

> And comes that other fall we name the fall.
> He says the highway dust is over all.

The rabbi at the funeral chapel had made the obligatory remarks concerning dust. It is no longer a problem to connect poor Sorkin at the end of his rope with these lines. Binstock writes slowly, with care:

> The bird would cease and be as other birds
> But that he knows in singing not to sing.

The strangest lines of all, these two. How do you not sing while singing? Perhaps you just sang more quietly, a lesser melody.

The question that he frames in all but words
Is what to make of a diminished thing.

Binstock sits back, the poem before him. It is as if he's just created it instead of simply copying it out to get it straight in his head. Everybody seemed to be writing this poem, singing this song these days. He remembered Tarloff, the company's third president in two years, taking him to lunch to say good-bye.

"It's not just that we're facing hard times, here at the firm or even here in America."

"No . . . ?"

"We're looking at a worldwide diminution of assets."

Tarloff's gnarled hands shaped—what? An apple? A melon?

"Just imagine, Lee, that this whole globe we live on was of a certain diameter—worth a certain amount—something so large, of course, no computer could even figure it out. And now it's just—shrunk." His hands collapsed to a smaller apple or melon. "The value of the whole world as we know it. Permanently. It was worth X in total. Now it's worth V. Simple as that."

Binstock had not asked if that was why they'd had to let him go. It was a lofty reason, very classy; but he was afraid it might come down to something not quite so elegant. It was perhaps not that the dollar value of the planet Earth had shrunk; more like the fact it was November, his end-of-the-year bonus would have been substantial—and Tarloff needed every penny to keep the place afloat. Or because Binstock had worked closely with Sorkin and Tarloff was afraid Binstock might be implicated in that mess. The firm didn't need one more arrest on the business pages of the *New York Times*. But instead of asking he'd just laughed nervously. And Tarloff had asked if Binstock had understood what he was saying and Binstock had said oh, yes, he understood it quite well.

• • •

HE WALKED BACK TO the bedroom, to the edge of the bed. Eugenia slept, lightly snoring, her sweet mouth pushed open and closed by the push and pull of breath. Binstock stood by the bed waiting, watching her breathe, anxious and grateful. When she woke he would tell her, "I saw Jenny Maslow this afternoon. I tried to find the poem in the library and I couldn't. Sorkin mixed up Sandburg and Frost and I figured Jenny would know."

She would say, "Oh?", noncommittal as usual in these matters. He was the one who was jealous of ex-husbands, ex-lovers. Eugenia lacked the jealous gene. For her, love and sex were one and entirely in the present.

He remembered their first sexual play, one, two, three times until one night she said, why always three, one good is better than three any which way. But forced or natural, he mourned the energy of youth which could play the games it wished— could push to the edge, foolish bravado or not.

GONE NOW WAS THEIR Italian driving all night on impulse in the warm rain, stopping in a hilltop town at midnight, the piazzas mysterious in the moonlight, the ubiquitous cats lurking around silent fountains, the pensiones all full or shut, the first one no, the second one no, the third pensione seedy but offering a room, the walls damp, the bed not made up, one towel for both of them, too exhausted for anything more interesting than sleep but holding each other anyway, almost too tired to make love so love made them, falling asleep on scratchy sheets the instant after. Later, of course, came the careful planning of travel, the well-planned reservations with the precisely specified rooms.

Eugenia rolled to her side; her eyelids fluttered. When she

saw him standing there she called out his name. Binstock sat down next to her. Eugenia laid her head on his chest and she suddenly shook with tears. He didn't know what to do except hold her and stupidly say, "What is it, what is it?"

She spoke between sobs as children do, hard to hear at first, almost a whisper, then louder and louder. "I thought there would be more time . . . I thought we would have a child, maybe two by now . . . I wanted to start a real magazine one day . . . *The Partisan Review, Vanity Fair,* I don't know what but not just a newsletter that tells everybody—stuff . . . I majored in literature not journalism . . . When my sister died so young I knew I would always feel less than before . . . everything is less than before . . . we make love less . . . we probably waited too long to start children and now maybe we can't . . . "

She lifted her head from his chest blinking at Binstock.

"Do you know," she said, "I had to start holding my head at a funny angle because I couldn't hear clearly with my left ear, do you know that was when I was only fourteen? I didn't tell you when we got married because I was ashamed to be losing such serious things still so young. I don't know which is a worse diminished thing—the body or the way the mind dreams and then gives up dreaming. For God's sake I'm thirty-eight. Isn't that too young for all this?"

She sobbed lightly, exhausted by her own emotions. "I knew about all that," he lied. "I just ignored it."

Binstock forgot about telling her about seeing Jenny, forgot about selling the clarinet, a dumb idea whose joy was just as dumb, just as temporary. Instead he held Eugenia tightly, miserable at hearing so many unspoken regrets.

After a few moments he got up and went to the end table and got the round metal ashtray which had not been used since he'd given up cigars two years ago—now as useless an object as his clarinet. He crumpled up the piece of paper on which he'd written the Frost poem and found his old lighter in a bureau drawer. It was mysterious, a morning flame inside their bedroom. Eugenia pulled herself up on one elbow and watched the poem burn into black and white and then into crumbs of black.

She murmured, "What are you doing?"

When he told her she nodded. Binstock watched her watching the embers. It was as if his wife had been his partner in writing the poem down in order to figure out what to make of it, as if copying and then burning poems was an ordinary event. She'd woken up, weeping variations on the same theme. The Oven Bird was a tough teacher. Sorkin had learned the hard way. Now it was their turn. Subtraction was the law and the sentence. Everything else was just a plea bargain.

AFTERWARDS BINSTOCK WAS STARVED, the way you are sometimes after a funeral or after making love. He and Eugenia covered the kitchen table with smoked salmon, cream cheese, breads, jams and had a feast.

"You know," she said, her mouth full and trying not to spill her coffee, "the important part, the part we sort of missed, is 'what to *make* of a diminished thing.' The ball, as we say when we play tennis, is in our court."

"Yes," Binstock said. His wounded mouth was a mass of pungent dough, the sharp taste of poppy seeds and sweet-smelling raspberry jam. "Yes," he said. "That's what the bird wants you to think."

A Man of Sorrows and Acquainted with Grief

Inspired by THE PASSION ACCORDING TO ST. JOHN
by Johann Sebastian Bach

Kraft was lost, there was no getting around it. For a half hour he'd gone from highways with exotic names—The Joe Halliburton Memorial Turnpike—to equally incomprehensible numbers, I-45, which turned into a local road numbered 635. Now instead of missed turnoffs and U-turns it was a matter of dirt roads loitering past rickety wooden shacks, chickens and other fowl, dogs dozing in front of a 7-11. The wrong side of whatever tracks his new home might boast.

He might have gotten himself lost because of the unfamiliarity of a Texas roadscape to a man whose eyes were entirely accustomed to cityscapes. His first wife, Yvette, had called him an unregenerate New Yorker. To which he replied, "Being a New Yorker is not a crime, you can't be unregenerate." "Maybe not," she said, "but it's a handicap. You didn't learn to drive till the age of thirty-three and you still can't read a map worth shit." Yvette had owned a tough mouth, in contrast to Maureen.

Still, it was gentle, soft-spoken Maureen who had landed him in his present predicament, lost on a highway, lost in Texas, a little lost in his own life. Maureen's skill with numbers had gotten her a job offer from a Texas bank so tasty it could not be turned down. Not by Maureen and thus not by Kraft, who wanted only to continue adjunct teaching two days a week at Pace University; to keep conducting the Bronx Community Orchestra—small potatoes but his own dish—while dreaming of doing the Mahler Eighth in Lincoln Center.

Maureen was only months past the awfulness of nursing a twin sister through a two-year soul-destroying illness when he'd met her. She was ripe for a change of heart, and a change of scene didn't seem too unattractive. Change, any change, promised some relief from remembered pain—though she kept it quiet, private. It was not a distancing that he minded. He and his first wife Yvette had been entwined in each other's souls, and when that kind of intimacy went bad it went very bad.

So change there would be; a life with more cash even sacrificing New York dash. And if there was to be a child, perhaps two, then the move to Texas seemed inevitable. Kraft was reconciled. Even in mid-April with the heat raging, even with the car's air-conditioning working on its own intermittent impulse, an occasional blast of cold air, then a downward spiral: cold, cool, warm. He'd pressed every button in sight but nothing changed.

He slipped a cassette into the rental car's tape deck. Music would ease the pain of a sweaty search for a gas station where he might get right-left instructions to get him back in the right direction. Right-left was what people who couldn't read maps used instead of cartography. Turn right at Bushwick, turn left at Gibson Court, and sooner or later you arrived at what he and Maureen were now to call home.

The sonority of the music surprised him, terrific bass, the treble lines never breaking or turning shrill, even under the stress of the mighty chorus of the Bach *St. John Passion*. The air-conditioning unit might be fragile but just listen to these woofers and tweeters. Did they have musicians consulting on the sound control at General Motors, standing around the factory wearing hard hats, examining blueprints the way engineers did in TV commercials? Somebody had arranged for a magnificent, blood-trembling opening chorus to fill the small cabin with the three-hundred-year-old pain and passion. Kraft found it thrilling. If he had to start living in the boredom of cars and white lines instead of subways, buses and the left-right of legs, and sweating out being lost, then the radio was an important anodyne.

Healing was how it felt. Kraft was submerged in the ecstatic curve of the chorus. *Herr unser Herrscher.* Lord our sovereign. . . . Echoes of poor Koerschner, lively, noisy Koerschner, and his greeting, "Well, Herr Kraft. Guten tag." Koerschner, step-by-step diminishing into an X-ray of his old substantial self, needing and accepting only the consolations of music and visits from grandchildren, the pleasures of his vast collections of recordings of birdsongs, all catalogued, all with unpronounceable names. When the hospital rabbi came around he would inveigle the poor man into a discussion of St. Thomas Aquinas and the logical proofs of the existence of God. Rabbi-baiting was one of Koerschner's old agnostic sports.

The death of your best friend was not the smoothest way to ease you out of your New York life, but that was the way it had gone. Kraft took in the numbers on the speedometer and clamped down on the brake. He'd had two speeding violations in the last six months. "Put it down to stress," Maureen said, to soften his anxiety, "moving, changing jobs."

"Tell that to the judge," Kraft said. A suspended driver's license in New York would have been an inconvenience; in Texas it was unimaginable, like losing a leg or an arm.

Restless, Kraft did some fast-forward tape-surfing. *Verherrlicht worden bist.* "You will be glorified," the chorus reminded Kraft, with a thrilling blast, and he pulled into a Shell station which offered a free car wash with every fill-up. The attendant was a red-haired local kid who pulled out a map and had to be convinced to put it away and just explain in surface terms—turn left here, right there.

Set straight, Kraft was eager to get back and talk to Maureen. It was almost five o'clock. His first meeting with the Floyd Robbins High School of Performing Arts had gone well. Everyone seemed thrilled to have the New York musician teaching their kids, conducting their orchestra. Even Basford, the cool "headmaster"—fancy term for a high school principal, probably to impress the parents. But Basford was pretty sophisticated. He and Kraft had chatted about Haydn's attitude towards Beethoven's counterpoint, things like that. Basford had a Ph.D. in musicology, a step up the ladder from Kraft; nevertheless Kraft took the lead in programming conversations.

They'd settled on the first concert. Familiar, safe sounds. This was a small city, conservative. He'd been reminded of this fact a number of times by one of the board members, an intense, serious man, white hair, half-glasses, familiar with Maynard Solomon's biography of Beethoven and the Haydn London Symphonies. He had one of those non–New York names Kraft was getting used to, Jordan Baines, a retired oil-zillionaire with a passion for music. He'd graduated NYU Law School and he and his wife visited New York once a year, without fail. They liked Jewish food, he told Kraft, who was somewhat dazed at receiving this information.

It had been quick and easy to arrive at a program for the kickoff concert: a Berlioz overture, the Benvenuto Cellini, then the Tchaikovsky Serenade for Strings, with the Haydn 102nd Symphony as the centerpiece. All were Kraft's choices, a happy school board and headmaster along for the ride. Tonight he and Maureen would celebrate, exchange battle stories from the new Texas wars, drink too much wine, go to bed early or at least swiftly.

Back on the antiseptic sweep of the Interstate highway the Bach swept him along, too. Kraft knew the St. John score well, had always wanted to conduct it, but there was never an opportunity, never any money for such a large chorus, for extra rehearsals. There came the exquisite aria for alto and two oboes, a moving mixture of middle-range and high-range sounds.

"What ze lay person cannot bear to believe," Koerschner had said in his slightly comic-opera mittel-Europe accent, as he lay in a confusion of hospital equipment, "is zat Bach was as concerned with solving ze technical problem of balancing an alto sound with ze soprano range of ze two oboes as much as wiz expressing ze suffering of Christ on ze cross. Zis is too professional. Zis they cannot accept." By this time Koerschner was having difficulty catching his breath at the end of so long a statement. Finally Kraft was reduced to writing notes to his friend in hopes that Koerschner would strain himself less by writing back, saving breath.

It was the mournful sifting of oboes and a rich and dark alto voice in the very aria they'd discussed that reminded Kraft of the last exchange of letters. Following the inexorable law that the living and healthy will bring their troubles to the sick and dying, he had written a letter which began as an apology for leaving New York for Texas when his friend, his teacher and mentor, was in trouble. But the letter quickly evolved into a lament for the slackness of Kraft's own life, the lack of forward movement, Leonard Bernstein, Toscanini in his soul and a high school conductor in his life.

Koerschner had written back (it was his last note): *I will miss you. I got to know you too late, this is painful. But I have done everything too late. I came to America too late, I started writing music too late. The only thing I'm doing too early is my current activity of departure.*

There are birdsongs in Texas where you go which I will now never hear, so beautiful, so surprising in their repetition. Birdsong is one of the luckiest gifts. It is painful to have to leave this extraordinary earth with its lucky gift of music, this extraordinary earth where, at one time or another, every kind of happiness seems possible.

Then addressing Kraft's personal anxiety: *Please remember: You are a good man, gifted and quick on the draw; your talent will be what you make of it, and wherever you use it. But in the meantime enjoy your life because it respects you.*

That last line haunted Kraft with its gnomic last phrase. How did a life respect its owner? Shouldn't it be the other way around? The aria ended and a mournful chorale filled the car. The round sounds of the Bach were a perfect accompaniment to his Koerschner memories; was it Bach's musical passion or his love of the Passion's Jesus that made it feel so healing, or maybe the two couldn't be split in spite of oboes and altos and crucifixions. Strange that it should help him say a sweaty good-bye to his friend in a Hertz rental car on an alien Interstate 45.

In the rear mirror Kraft became gradually aware of a whirling rainbow on top of the car behind him. Oh, shit, he thought, afraid to look at the speedometer. Ninety, he'd been going ninety. He braked gradually and pulled over to the shoulder, dizzy, afraid.

He was already opening the glove compartment, fiddling for the registration and insurance stuff when he saw the trooper looming in his side mirror, very tall, very wide; it was like seeing a house moving towards you, about to crush you. Behind the shiny black belt and boots, the holster and protruding brown gun butt, Kraft saw one edge of the police car front bumper—a sticker read: I FOUND JESUS. SHOULDN'T YOU BE LOOKING?

The trooper bent over and rapped on the window. In his panic Kraft had forgotten to roll it down. He hit the button but he had also forgotten to turn off the tape deck and now, through the downward slide of the window, a chorus blasted out. In return, the heat blasted in, taking Kraft's breath away.

The policeman squinted at Kraft over this beautiful racket. He seemed bewildered to be greeted by the volume of the music and the foreign words. For an instant Kraft sensed he might have the advantage, might escape this disaster, license intact, mobile, he and Maureen safe, happy in their new, two-car world. Before the trooper could say a word Kraft took his life in his hands, in his mouth and voice. He had to almost shout to be heard over the music.

"Listen, officer, I know I was going over the speed limit . . . but I was absolutely carried away, wiped out by the music and I had no idea what the numbers on the speedometer said . . . not just the music but the words, the meaning . . . I mean it's almost Easter time and I was so moved, I lost myself. . . . Listen . . ." Kraft chanted along with the thundering chorus—he'd done this so many times in the classroom—

> *Christus der selig macht,*
> *Kein Bos's hat begangen,*
> *Der ward fur uns in der Nacht . . .*

The policeman owned a beefy face, red-cheeked with puffy pink lips, now all frozen in a stare of astonishment. Finally he spoke. "What's that language? Some kind of Jewish?"

"It's German. It means . . ." To stop shouting Kraft turned the volume down. "It means: *Christ who brings us salvation, himself innocent of any sin, was seized in the night like a thief . . .*" Afraid to leave the word thief hanging in the air, Kraft stumbled forward, pulling from some part of his memory more words he needed. *"He was despised and rejected, a man of sorrows and acquainted with grief."* That felt a lot better. "The pain and beauty of it broke me up and I lost control of who I was, where I was, of what I was doing." Thinking, well it's a little true, Koerschner and music and suffering and Christ had gotten all mixed up in the flow of music and memory.

The trooper pushed his Texas-style hat back from his damp forehead. He was silent for a long moment. Then he said, "Would you get out of the car please, sir."

Oh my God, Kraft thought, sweat blurring his eyes. He clicked a swift slideshow in his mind: being bent over the car, being searched for weapons, for drugs. He closed the door quietly. His head came about to the trooper's shoulders. The air trembled with heat. Without warning the policeman grabbed him and hugged him to his chest. No man had held him that close since his grandfather. Dizzy with astonishment, with fear, Kraft registered the smell of sweat and something minty, chewing gum, mouthwash, something.

"You," the trooper said into his ear. "You're my brother."

"What?"

"You're my brother—my brother in Jesus."

Thank God, Kraft thought. No ticket, no suspended license. The trooper stepped back and stared at Kraft. A smile creased his mouth. "Would you get back in the car please, sir?"

Kraft focused his eyes on a pin on the man's chest. It read Art Birdwell. Giddy with anxiety he thought, for one stupid second, together we make Art and Kraft—brothers, indeed. He was afraid to look back. He imagined Art Birdwell's bulk sliding into the patrol car, his mouth moving, radioing something to somebody—maybe checking to see if his newfound brother in Jesus had a criminal record, was driving a stolen car.

In a few minutes he was back. He looked triumphant. "May I see your driver's license and your proof of insurance, sir." He pronounced it *in*surance with the accent on the first syllable. Kraft's father, Louis, had been an insurance broker for thirty-five years, always with the accent on the second syllable.

His son Ben took this as proof that he was now in a foreign country.

Kraft scrambled to hand the documents over. Then the wait, staring straight ahead, his shirt sticking to his back, pitying, relieved drivers whizzing by on the highway. He turned the tape volume up and Bach sang again. Now it was about plaiting a crown of thorns and calling to Jesus, in mockery, Hail, King of the Jews.

A different kind of panic at what he might have started grew in Kraft and he turned the music off, as if that might let him start over again. But when Trooper Birdwell reappeared at his window his heart sank. The man wore a grin as wide as his chest. He stuck a beefy hand through the window and handed back Kraft's license and the insurance card.

"Well, Brother Kraft," he said. "You were going twenty-five miles over the speed limit. But if y'all would come down to the station and just tell some of our people there what you told me—I mean about the amazing gift of light that came to you through the music about Our Lord—well, I think you can count on a touch more mercy than justice from our fair city. The boys'r all real eager to hear your story."

Kraft did not move.

Birdwell stared down at him with the bluest eyes Kraft had ever seen.

"Y'all will be good enough to share your experience with the rest of us, ain't that right?"

Kraft did not speak. A life of glibness, of quick improvising, was suddenly gone.

"Mr. Kraft"—the question of brotherhood seemed to be suspended for the moment—"This is ya third moving violation . . ."

Kraft came alive. "It's not that, officer," he said. "It's just very personal. I mean feelings like that . . ."

"Ah understand. But if more people shared the coming of the light, it could be a different world down here."

Kraft folded. "Sure, I'll be happy to tell about it. How do I get—"

The door opened and Trooper Birdwell said, "Just scoot over and I'll get us down to the station real quick."

Kraft had said almost nothing since singing his first terrified half-lie, the swift riff which had rolled off his tongue to save his ass. It was an old habit, a childhood style of survival—he was as quick with words as with notes, a good sight reader and a good liar when threatened: a bad report card, a lost expensive pair of gloves, a missed piano lesson. But the weirdness of the situation he'd talked himself into had temporarily silenced him. With his car about to be invaded he found a voice again.

"What about your car?" he jerked his head backwards.

"Not a problem. Brother Cartwright will lead us back to the station."

Kraft twisted around. There at the wheel was Brother Cartwright, a skinny, smiling trooper, sans hat, waving a greeting; a second witness to his perjury. Kraft scooted over to the passenger side, endangering his testicles since there was a gear shift on the floor to be negotiated; but Trooper Birdwell was looming and Kraft scuttled.

The siren behind him began its furious whine and the whirling light resumed. Startled, Kraft jumped and hit his head. Trooper Birdwell turned the key and said, "Seat belt, sir. State law." Breathing the new aroma of sweat and mint that filled the car, Kraft buckled his seat belt. It was just as well because the law apparently knew no speed limits in Texas. The difference between an Interstate highway and a roller coaster had apparently not been revealed to Trooper Art Birdwell or to Brother Cartwright, who was clearing their way, whirling rainbow, moaning siren and all.

"Let's get us some air," Birdwell said. He hit a couple of buttons and a blast of life-giving cool air rolled over Kraft's soaking face and chest. While he huddled in his passenger seat, trying to control his urge to throw up, Art Birdwell spoke revelations.

"What happened to y'all back there, goin' outta control blinded by the light . . ." Kraft could see the experience was turning mythical in Art Birdwell's hands; there was no knowing how far it might go. ". . . It's like what happened to me right after little Billy was squashed like a bug right in front of our house. A drunken sumbitch drivin' an eighteen-wheeler took my Billy boy and Sally and I were in the darkness that knows no end for I don't know how long." He squinted a look of misery at Kraft. "But the mystery was just at the beginning. We found His mercy and we've been wrapped in His arms ever since. We know the joy of the Lamb." Tears wet the leathery face and Kraft felt sick at his stomach for reasons that had nothing to do with hairpin turns or jamming brakes. What kind of a disgusting fraud had he started, with a man whose suffering was real and whose Jesus was equally real?

Talking and weeping in an odd singsong, Art Birdwell said, "I forgave that drunken sumbitch the way He would have, the way you would have, Brother Kraft."

I would have killed the bastard, Kraft thought. He would have given anything to go back to the moment on the highway, hand over his insurance card and registration, take his ticket, lose his license, confess to an angry Maureen that he was now helpless, would have to be driven everywhere like a child, that their new beginning had been blighted by an absent-minded love of Bach on Interstate 45. But he had nothing to offer in exchange for such a miracle.

● ● ●

SOMEBODY AT THE 12TH Precinct seemed to have forgotten where the buttons for air-conditioning were. The tall, dirty windows were tightly shut and there was a sort of hum in the air, but the temperature was tropical. A serious sense of unreality walked with Kraft through the doors—maybe it was the slow-revolving ceiling fans, or the two dogs, a black Lab sleeping on folded paws, the other a slender, elegant Doberman, growling softly, as if talking to himself; maybe it was the way Brother Cartwright introduced him to the assembled group of troopers as an Easter Lamb who'd been saved on Interstate 45 by St. John, or finding himself blinded by the light of a camera flash—there was a newspaperman covering the precinct. He actually wore a white suit and the sense of unreality Kraft was caught in resolved itself into late-night memories of thirties movies with Texas Ranger hats (they seemed not to have changed in style since those movies were made), pistols protruding from hip and shoulder holsters, sweating reporters in white suits, and slowly-turning ceiling fans.

Art Birdwell must have been pushed to preacherlike eloquence on his car radio because a welcoming committee was waiting. Kraft was asked to sing the same song he'd sung in a sudden frenzy with the flashing lights in the rearview mirror urging him on. Only now the song had new words; the rapture at hearing the pain of the Passion couldn't be recaptured precisely. Being encircled by eager, interested faces, by a reporter scribbling, it became an aria of Easter and its mysteries.

He had no idea when Easter was this year, only that it came shortly before Passover because his sister had invited him and Maureen for the Seder in Cambridge and Maureen's mother had invited them for Easter Sunday dinner in Chicago, neither being possible because of Maureen's new job, Kraft's teaching and rehearsal schedule and the high cost of the plane tickets. But it didn't matter. Easter became an image, a way of escape, a shortcut to get himself out of this mess, back for dinner with Maureen, this awful, sweating day behind him, ready to start again, clean, all of it forgotten, not least of all Trooper Birdwell's angry tears at the sumbitch who had crushed his Billy Boy like a bug.

THREE-QUARTERS OF AN HOUR later, driving back, Kraft heard it on the radio. Every bit of it, as if it were real news—a New York driver seeing the light on the Interstate, hearing the Good News for the first time in his life. They even gave his full name, Mr. Benjamin Kraft, and his job at the Floyd Robbins High School of Performing Arts. He switched stations but there it was on several of the others. It was drive time and surely some of the school board would have heard it. Maureen would probably have heard, too. Like Kraft, she could not stand the boredom of driving without the radio or the tape deck on. What kind of town was this where a foolish traffic incident could become news! The Bible Belt, everyone knew the expression. Kraft had always assumed it was in the South, but he had only a vague idea of where. Geography had never been his strong point.

SHE WAS SITTING IN the tiny kitchen, at the fold-down breakfast table, tapping at her laptop. She looked up, startled; a sheen of hair veiled her eyes. Maureen's red hair was a great feature; long and blindingly red, frequently in her eyes. He leaned over her and kissed her mouth. If she knew what had happened, Kraft was sure she would wait for him to say something. There was something hidden, something once removed, about Maureen's emotional responses. He would tease her about what he called her buried life and she would laugh him off, saying the whole world is not Hungarian, not Jewish, not so expressive at all times.

"How's the job? They say the second week's the worst. The first week is a daze. By the second the reality takes over."

"I think Small loves me. That's what I call reality." Small was the chief financial officer who had recruited her. "I'm already doing the numbers on a leveraged buyout. From down here. Hard to believe."

He sank into a chair. "This air-conditioning is wonderful. I couldn't get it to work right in the car."

"A lot of odd things seemed to happen in that car."

"You heard."

"It was all over the radio."

"It'll be in the papers tomorrow."

"I almost drove onto the shoulder when I heard your name—what happened? I mean it's so far from you . . ."

He told her the truth, that he had surprised the hell out of himself by being desperate to save his driver's license, by reaching for any story that offered salvation.

"It was the bumper sticker that triggered it. If it had read GUNS DON'T KILL PEOPLE, PEOPLE KILL PEOPLE, maybe I would have spun out a story about how I was new in town and daydreaming about needing a gun to protect my family, I don't know. Also the air-conditioning wasn't working. The car was like a steam bath. You don't make rational decisions at a moment like that."

He opened the refrigerator and scanned the interior, suddenly starved.

"Well," Maureen said. "It was a brilliant idea. It got you off the hook."

He turned around, pained, anxious for her to understand.

"It was a disgusting idea. I mean, not if somebody had really felt that way, but to use it for a trick—" And he told her of Trooper Birdwell's little boy and his talking about being wrapped in His mercy and the joy of the Lamb while weeping and driving like a witch on a broomstick. "I went from feeling triumphant to feeling like shit in about two seconds."

"I'm sorry," she said. "You didn't mean to humiliate the man. And he doesn't know." She gazed at him in a steady way that made Kraft uncomfortable.

"That's just it," he says. "Nobody knows except us. The whole town's going to have an idea about me that I don't know how to handle."

"You'd better close the refrigerator door," Maureen said. "I've got a fresh salmon in there for tonight."

Kraft remembered. "And I've got a bottle of wine in the car. How'd you like a nice boiled Chardonnay for dinner?" He raced out to the car. By the time they ate, the Chardonnay was cold and the salmon was indeed fresh and tasty. Kraft was feeling better about life with his new wife in this new ticky-tacky home, in this new city. They had rented sight unseen because of the rush to get Maureen started on her new job and because it was easier to take a blind chance than to spend the air fare for a reconnaissance visit. They talked of plans for a new house; the next one would be larger—code word for a child or two or three.

Kraft was feeling loosened up. He'd had more wine than usual, enough to fuel a difficult question to Maureen.

"You were looking at me, before, in a different way," he said. "What were you thinking?"

"When?"

"Before."

Right after Maureen had reminded him that nobody, not Birdwell, not anybody, knew about the day's religious fakery except them, she had leveled that intense, steady gaze at him. Kraft was certain they both remembered the moment but Maureen did not seem to want to get into it. He dropped it and pulled her up from her chair and her sorbet and cookies thinking bed might be nicer than analyzing difficult gazes.

They left the dishes, the pans, everything—even though Maureen's cardinal rule was that after fish you washed it all right away or you had fish smells forever. But it was an inauguration, the first time they'd made love in their new place, city, state, life. It had been too hectic and exhausting the first ten days and this evening they made languorous love, made love instead of explaining gazes, instead of feeling remorse. It was fine and afterwards he fell asleep, his head on her stomach, swathed in Maureen's long red hair, breathing the sweet smell of her shampoo.

KRAFT WOKE, ALONE IN the bed, groggy and feeling wrong about something. Not something large, he knew at once; something small. As he swam from sleep to the morning he'd been hearing a phrase of music, but it was the words that were the matter, not the melody. *He was a man of sorrows and acquainted with grief.* He'd thrown that at Trooper Birdwell as an extra weapon.

He should have known he was making a hodgepodge of references. It wasn't even Bach. It was from the *Messiah.* He heard in his mind's ear the old Marian Anderson recording Koerschner had once given him, a birthday present, heard again the way she bent the notes, infusing melodic curve with sonorous sympathy. He was des*pis-ed,* re*jected.* A man of sorrows and acquainted with grief. That last phrase had always struck him as an amazing line of poetry: *acquainted* with grief. Not submerged by grief, not destroyed by grief; acquainted. The casualness of the word gave the pain its power.

This settled, he turned to find Maureen. She often slipped out of bed before him and woke him for breakfast. This morning the air was empty of the usual coffee and toast smells.

Kraft swung out of bed but the ringing of the phone put his search on hold.

It was Jordan Baines, formerly of oil and now of Haydn, Beethoven and Jewish cooking. Baines's phone had been ringing off the hook— members of the school board. Everybody was thrilled.

"Sorry to call so early, Ben."

"No, no . . ."

"But there's so much fuss goin' on. Now please understand—wouldn't want to trespass on a man's private feelings but just want you to know that the board would be most happy if you'd switch the first program. Do the *St. John Passion*. Whole town'll come out for that, now. We could fill the basketball court 'stead of the school concert hall."

Kraft stalled, he mentioned the extra rehearsal time, the technical demands of the Passion.

"The concert date's awful close to Easter Sunday. Be sort of perfect," Jordan Baines said. He held a pause, then: "I think most everybody was truly moved by the things you said. Take a look at this morning's paper. Doesn't happen every day, a revelation like yours, speedin' down the highway. If Saint Paul'd been drivin' a car on the road to Damascus . . . Hah . . . Anyways, you think about it, Ben. Let me know."

Kraft folded his head in his hands but the night's sweet shampoo smell of Maureen's hair was so strong that it conquered even his confusion at what he'd started. He found her in the walk-in closet downstairs, intensely searching through some of their still unpacked luggage. She was wearing her nightgown but her face, when she turned it up at his approach, was shadowed under the eyes, dark creases at the corners of her mouth. She looked awful.

"Are you okay?" he said, feeling it a dumb but necessary question.

She upended a small carrying case, a fountain of sunglasses, handkerchiefs and old ballpoint pens.

"I couldn't sleep much," she said.

"Why?"

She scavenged a hard-sided piece of luggage, tops and bottoms of pajamas, shoes in velvet drawstring bags. "Damn." She looked over her shoulder at Kraft. "I couldn't get it out of my mind. What you said, what I heard on the radio about Christ who brings us salvation, innocent himself . . ."

"But that was just Bach . . ."

"And most of all, he was a man of sorrows and acquainted with grief." She pulled down a large case and almost beaned herself and Kraft with it. When she tried to open it, it stuck. "Give me a hand, Ben, please."

He remembered the combination, it was her birthdate, and it came open. "What are you looking for? What's so important? God, what time did you get up? Did you have breakfast?"

"I'm looking for a hat. I got up at three."

"Three o'clock in the Ayem? Why did that stuff yesterday upset you so much? I don't get it, Maureen. I had a crazy day—but I slept."

She turned a wan smile. "You always sleep," she said. "You're an artist of sleep."

He rubbed his eyes. "If Jordan Baines hadn't called I'd still be sacked out."

He told her about Baines and the suggested program change.

"Do you want to do it?" she asked.

"I don't think so. These kids are pretty good but they're not up to the St. John. And it would be like—an endorsement of the whole thing. You don't capitalize on something that was supposed to be a joke—a kind of ugly joke but still a joke." He took a beat. "But I have to admit, I get a charge out of the idea of conducting those sublime choruses."

"Very grand." She smiled.

"Grandiose," he said.

She gave him a kind of echo of the gaze that had troubled him last night over the Chardonnay.

"And that's not for you?" she asked.

"I don't know," Kraft said. "I think Papa Haydn's my man. Listen, I'm worried about you up since three. And I've never seen you wear a hat."

"You've only known me for two years or so. You have to expect a few surprises. And never mind Papa Haydn. *You're* my man. Not to worry." She kissed him quickly and went back to her search.

Just two years! He'd met her a few months after the death of her twin sister. Maureen had sweated through four years of her sister's failing heart; had taken the years before turning twenty and given them to seeing her out, finishing college two years late. It was not something she could talk about. The friend who introduced them had told Kraft or he never would have known about it. It may have been the reason he'd felt in her, practically at their first date, large silences, secret recesses not even their quick intimacy could touch.

Kraft was no stranger to loss, his mother dead at forty-five of cancer and his father selling insurance North, East, South, West so that a grudging Aunt Rose became mother and father. His ambition, too, was woven with a sense of loss: a good pianist but not quite concert level, a talented conductor but finally destined for high school orchestras instead of Rome, Paris, London. "Zere are twenty-five major conductors in ze whole musical world," Koerschner's not-quite-consoling words. "Better to make peace and do good work wherever you are." And there was his first marriage—Yvette. He'd hidden hopes there, too, and they'd been lost.

"Aha!" Maureen turned to him wearing a foolish-looking beige hat. "What do you think?"

"You look like a flapper."

"It was called a cloche when my mother bought it for me."

Apprehensive, Kraft said, "I don't think it looks so great on you."

"Don't forget, I won't be wearing it with a nightgown in church. A dress, shoes, gloves, a hat. You know. I need a mirror." She vanished and returned before Kraft could organize his reactions to what she'd said. Maureen didn't go to church. They'd agreed their childhood religions meant little to them. Their children could pick their own when the time came. It had all been talked through.

"This'll do," she said. "Come on, I'll make us some breakfast."

She set out the orange juice, the plates, made French toast and coffee, dressed in slippers, her nightgown and the beige cloche hat. Kraft waited for a mouthful of French toast and then mumbled, "You're going to church, today?"

"I think so," she said.

"But I thought that was all—done with."

"I thought so, too. Then after you fell asleep I couldn't get what you said, what you did, out of my head. I kept wondering why you would use that particular strategy on the unsuspecting police. Maybe you felt more than you knew, yourself."

"Oh, my God, Maureen."

She ignored how flustered the conversation was making him. "I'm not being literal," she said, pouring coffee for both of them with a steady hand. "I don't think you found Christ in spite of yourself, or any of that, I mean something more subtle—the feelings behind the capture of Jesus, his sacrifice—I've heard the *St. John Passion.* Those feelings are all in there."

"You're mixing up the words and the music. Any feelings I had came from the music. Maureen, darling Maureen, this is your childhood, not anything to do with me. I was just fighting a panic attack at the idea of a third violation and I saw—"

"I know," she said. "You saw the bumper sticker. Anyway, I found myself, in the middle of the night, with a ferocious desire to set foot in church again. To hear the words of the Mass. I looked up the Yellow Pages and found a Catholic church here in Baptist land." She stood up and started to push her flood of red hair under the hat, as if she were off to church that moment, in slippers and nightgown.

"Be a good soul and clean up the breakfast mess while I get dressed. It's going to be a rush and they gave me directions but I have to allow time to get lost."

She started off but Kraft caught up to her and turned her around. When she turned, her hair twirled and Kraft caught a whiff of perfume, shampoo, soap, he had no idea. He just felt at that moment how glad he was to have found her. There was a tightness in his chest that was either angina or love.

"Maureen, why are you doing this?" he said, helpless.

Maureen paused and repeated the gaze that had troubled him the night before. She slowed down the pace of her talk as if to finally meet Kraft halfway in his anxiety.

"At three-thirty in the morning I couldn't stop thinking about my sister Peg and all she went through and how hard it is to say good-bye and how unfair because she was the one with all the pizzazz, all the zip, and she was taken."

Kraft was afraid she might start to cry. He didn't know what to say, was afraid he might never know what to say to meet such feelings.

Maureen took off the silly hat and poked at it, trying to give it some shape again and she said, "I haven't had any place to put my grieving, Ben."

"Into life—this life, ours . . ."

"It doesn't always work too well."

He would like to have held her, then, but it didn't seem fair to the depth of her unhappiness; embraces could be as glib as quick, improvised replies. Instead he said, "You kept it under wraps so much. I didn't know how you really felt, what you'd been through till maybe a few months ago. Not even a picture of her anywhere."

"I know." She managed a small smile. "It's my way. It's not you. It's just—everything."

She carried the hat out of the kitchen saying, "You'll clean up while I dress, hon. You promised." And she was gone. He hadn't promised but Kraft set about clearing the dishes, cold water for the stuff with eggs, hot water for the jellied plates.

From the corner of his eye he saw the light on the answering machine blinking. In the heat of the day, actual and otherwise, neither of them had checked for messages. Kraft hit the play button. It was his sister, Sarah, calling from Cambridge. Sarah, the smart sister, hare to his tortoise, calling to see how the East-erners were doing in the Southwest, calling to renew the invitation for Passover; the kids would love to see them. She was off for an endowed lecture on Wittgenstein at Oxford next week but please call back today. He thought how funny that he and Maureen had both been handed sisters they felt had more piz-zazz, more zip.

He used the portable phone and called Cambridge. In a matter, it seemed, of seconds, Kraft surprised himself by pouring out the highway encounter and its aftermath. Without a beat, Sarah took the story in her own direction.

"You're a real character, brother-mine," she said. "The *St. John Passion*. That's the one with the controversial text."

"What do you mean?"

"It's famous. The anti-Semitic one. You know—blame it on the Jews—what happened to Jesus. I know some people, not necessarily Jews, won't go to a performance, or they've been known to walk out."

"I never heard—"

"I had a friend," Sarah said, "who was applying for a job—arts administration, some fancy Jewish Y with poetry readings and an orchestra of their own. During the interview they asked her if she'd agree with their decision not to perform the *St. John Passion*. Because of the text. Excoriating the Jews instead of the Romans and so forth. She said, 'What about the *St. Matthew Passion*? That was as bad or worse. "Let it be on our heads and on our children." ' No, she wouldn't agree—she told them she thought Bach was Bach. She got the job, anyway."

"Oh, my God." He was quiet for a long moment or two.

"What? Ben, are you okay?"

He was not up to telling her about Maureen, the hat, the Catholic church. Instead, he let out something he didn't know was boiling up. "What the hell is all this stuff? What do you mean I'm a real character? I know you're in Cambridge and I'm only in a special Arts high school in a small city in Texas, but what's the point of rubbing this business in my face, now of all times? Are you telling me all Christians are anti-Semitic? That if I'm moved by the music, if I perform the St. John, that I'm stupidly ignoring my enemies? For God's sake, you remind me of Yvette and her wiseass talk. I thought I'd heard the last of that."

In response Sarah offered a long silence. Kraft broke it. "Hey," he said. "I'm on edge. Don't listen to me."

Sarah's voice was flat, saddened. She rode past his outburst. "You never answered about Passover? The kids want to see you."

"It doesn't look likely. You know—Maureen and I both have new jobs. And thanks for the story, kiddo."

He sat down at the still-uncleared table, the portable phone still in his hand. He couldn't believe he'd compared his sister to his first wife. He remembered their trip to northern Italy and the exquisite St. Sebastian in the Ca D'oro in Venice. Tintoretto, he thought, not certain. But what he clearly remembered was how moved he had been in the little church in Assisi with the perfect simple Christs by Giotto covering the walls. They had been on one of those teacher's tours, special rates, even lower for a winter trip, finding themselves snowbound in the lofty austerity of Perugia and then in the modest confines of Assisi. The sudden soft sifting of snow had practically closed down the little town. But the chapel was walking distance from the hotel, if you walked carefully, so there was something interesting you could do.

He remembered gazing with astonishment at the walls on which Giotto had sketched a cartoon version of ultimate, simple goodness. He remembered how a small line of monks had appeared out of some hidden part of the church and begun to sing a service. It sounded vaguely Gregorian or at least modal, and the hushed mood of esthetic worship was made perfect, as if the monks had been sent for that purpose. He remembered Yvette, keeping her hands warm with her little fur muff out of Tolstoy, the rest of her cool, ironic, saying, "This Jesus I think I went to school with. You know, the one who was a nice kid but slower than the rest. The one they made fun of at recess."

It was the wrong moment for her cleverness, it brought him down. Yvette was nothing if not clever, and she knew wrong moments from right, but the marriage had been coming apart, leaving bits and pieces in beds and restaurants in cities all over the north of Italy, and her elegant timing was suddenly gone.

Kraft had ignored her and had turned towards the line of monks chanting devotions, curious. They were the expected assortment of young and middle-aged Italian men, about a dozen of them, holding prayer books which held their total attention. But one monk caught his eye, a startling Xerox of his father, Louis Kraft, rotund, wearing a brown floor-length robe with a tasseled cord instead of the familiar white terry cloth bathrobe; it was Louis, entire. God, why was he seeing his father here of all places? Louis the absent father, the professional skeptic, even during the infrequent, obligatory visits to the synagogue. He had died a year before, of a sudden stroke, taking all the unfinished angers between father and son with him. Were they to be reopened here in a twelfth-century chapel in a frozen Assisi?

Kraft was tempted to whisper something of this to Yvette, but she had burned a few too many bridges that week and now that afternoon and he said nothing. Then, with the unexpected magic of such moments, the ersatz Louis Kraft, the Italian monk standing about six feet away from him, looked up from his prayer book, missal, whatever it was Catholics used, wet his thumb with a quick swipe across his tongue and used the moistened digit to turn the page. It was a perfect replay of a gesture Kraft had seen his father perform on a thousand Rosh Hashanas and Yom Kippurs, the young Kraft sandwiched between his father and his grandfather, constantly losing his place in the ancient Hebraic chant, his father thumb-moistening page after page to bring his son to the right place.

The moment had turned so real as to become comic. Kraft cracked the spell, pointing out the monk/father to Yvette and they both fell into laughter as soon as they were outside in the frozen sunlight. A half-hour later he and Yvette were getting pleasantly bombed over lunch in a trattoria near the town square, ready for sensual play before dinner in the queen-sized bed at the hotel, ready for a talk that would turn intense, angry over dinner, ready for the series of little talks and big talks which would lead them far away from the cartoon goodness of Giotto to the hopeless years of confusion which would end only when Maureen arrived—kind, loving, without irony, safe.

When she reappeared in the kitchen she was like a vision from a children's book: wine-colored dress, white gloves, beige hat, beige shoes, a Bible and her purse in her hands. She carried a white jacket.

"I spoke to Sarah," he said. "She called. I told her we probably couldn't make Passover there."

Maureen nodded. "How do I look?"

Kraft told the truth. "Like an unconventional beauty tamed into a conventional style."

"You're too clever for me," she said and laughed, truly laughed, for the first time that day. "Is that good or bad?"

"Like a pretty girl on her way to church," he said. "Is that better?"

"Better. It's my first Mass in five years."

"Not since—?"

"Yes."

Kraft thought, death, loss, mourning. The same things that can make you give up faith seemed to be the same things that can bring it on.

"I know this isn't fun for you," Maureen said.

"Well, I thought we had all this worked out."

"I thought so too."

She opened her purse and fiddled with a makeup case. "It was the things you said to the cop—they made me start thinking about how I used to feel when I went to Sunrise Mass on Easter morning with my mother. How consoled, how—shielded. And I couldn't forget, 'A man of sorrows,' you said. 'And acquainted with grief.' "

"I was wrong," he said, helpless, irrelevant. "It's not from the Passion. It's Handel—the *Messiah*. Not Easter. It's usually Christmas."

She slipped the white jacket over her dress and turned to face him. "Ben, I've been acquainted with grief."

"More than acquainted, Maureen. There aren't many things worse than what you lost."

The word "lost" tasted pallid on his tongue. What must it have been like watching a twin sister's heart fail for four years, stopping her own clock, then starting to live again with half a heart.

"Yes," she said. "Maybe so."

"But my God, Maureen, I was just playing a foolish trick."

She was outlining her mouth with lipstick now; a red slash against white skin. "I know," she said. "Your trooper Birdwell took it one way. I just want to see which way I'm going to take it." She kissed him a light good-bye, careful not to smudge her lipstick. "When I met you," she said, "it never occurred to me I'd be spending the rest of my life with you. You were a musician, you were broke, you made me laugh, you were supposed to be just for fun. But here we are. When you start things, you can't always know where they're going to end, can you?"

LATER HE PUT TOGETHER his scores for the *St. John Passion* and the Haydn 102nd just to be safe and was ready to head out for the school. He was not in the greatest mood to face his first rehearsal. It was only a run-through—whether of the Bach or the Haydn. A get acquainted session. But some of these students had passed statewide competitions to get into this school—the cream of the fiddlers, cellists, wind players. He would have to be up, at his best, not full of floating anxieties. Conducting was like teaching, you had to be keen, feel prepared. You couldn't have even a fraction of your mind elsewhere.

Instead, Kraft recalled, from nowhere, his father at the end. Louis Kraft had become the president of the synagogue after a life of ironic pseudo-observance. The rabbi wanted to take Louis's confession, had asked Kraft if he could come to the house. It had astonished agnostic, ignorant Kraft that Jews might do deathbed confessions, a ritual he'd assumed was confined to Catholics. It turned out that very orthodox Jews did. He repeated the rabbi's request to his father, who had never liked the man, a Lubovitcher the synagogue had hired over his objections. Louis Kraft considered the idea for a moment, then said, from behind closed eyes, "Fuck him. The golden rule is all you need." He slipped off an hour later.

The memory made Kraft laugh a little, which was what he needed to get himself going. The morning newspaper was lying on the doorstep, rolled up with a rubber band around it. He carefully stepped over it and left it lying there.

THE AUDITORIUM WAS SPANKING new, the oak paneling shining and smelling of wood polish. It had a name, of course: The Joe Halliburton Memorial Hall. Everything here was named after some oil and gas prodigy: halls, buildings, seats in the auditorium, endowed chairs, concert series. The orchestra was assembling onstage; violins were being polished, resin slid along horsehair, oboists whittled reeds endlessly, horn players belched out low testing blasts, violists ran scales and light timpani taps sat beneath it all. It was always a happy moment for Kraft.

On a tall wooden stool he surveyed his small, personal kingdom. Eighty-five or so young people, many of them Asian, a sprinkling of Hispanics, a black trumpet player. In a few weeks he would know them all by name, would know their idiosyncrasies, their special gifts, limitations. This was the beginning.

At his right, the first cellist was trying to get his attention. She wore a name pin, the kind Officer Birdwell had worn: Melanie Rutherford. Kraft motioned for her to step up to the podium. Holding her cello behind her, she stood and said, "Doctor Kraft, I just wanted to tell you I'm thrilled at the opportunity of playing the cello solo in the St. John."

"I see," Kraft said. "You mean 'Es Ist Vollbracht.' It Is Finished."

"Yes, sir."

If she knew then they all knew. School scuttlebutt by now.

"But we're scheduled to play the Haydn London Symphony. The D major."

She actually blushed. "I read about it in the paper," she said, her cello tilted against her breasts. "And it said you would conduct the *St. John Passion* because—anyway my teacher Mr. Fowler called me and said to start practicing it because it was so hard to melt the cello voice with the soprano . . ."

"It's a duet with the contralto," he said.

She was too embarrassed to go on. They all assume they know the whole story, Kraft thought. I'm the only one who doesn't.

"Melanie," he said. "I'm not sure if the Passion will be practical for this first season." He paused.

"I'm also the librarian," she said. "So I have to know what parts to put out."

He stalled. "You don't have any accent that I can hear. Are you from Texas?"

At the back of the auditorium a cellular phone trilled. A young man's voice called, heavy with the bent inflections of the South, "Dr. Kr-a-eft"—every teacher in Texas was apparently called Dr. It made Kraft nervous at the same time as furnishing a small, illicit pleasure—"Mr. Basford would lahk to see you in his office."

Melanie laid her cello down carefully against her chair. "I'm from Indiana," she said. "Terre Haute."

IT WAS UNPLEASANT FROM the moment Kraft saw Jordan Baines sitting next to Basford's desk in a halo of cigarette smoke. More meddling was coming up. To make it worse, he knew they would not get to the matter at hand until a round of civilities had been worked through. It was a style Kraft sort of enjoyed—but not today, precisely not today. In the middle of Basford asking him how his wife was taking to life in Texas, Kraft said, "What brings you to the school today, Mister Baines?"

"Jordan," Baines said. "Mister Baines is my father. Fact is, you didn't sound all that sympathetic to the change in programming I suggested this mornin'. I am concerned."

"I'm not too happy at using the school concert to illustrate an idea people may have about me."

Basford stepped in quickly. "You know, Ben, there is a tradition of timing school concerts to events in the secular calendar and the Christian year. In the Middle Ages that was often the only way ordinary people tracked the flow of the year."

"The banks all give out calendars these days," Kraft said. "We agreed on a program: Berlioz, Tchaikovsky and the Haydn one-oh-two, the D major. There's no reason to change it."

Baines stood up, tall, graceful with success. He leaned towards Kraft for emphasis. "Surely, Ben, you will not deny that you have set this town a bit on its ear with a revelation of religious feeling made first to a police officer and then to the media. A revelation having a great deal to do with the crucifixion of our Lord Jesus Christ."

"As expressed in the music of Bach," Kraft said as firmly as he could manage. "It should be no surprise to anyone that I'm someone mainly moved by music."

"Nicely put," Basford said quickly. "Of course the synergy of music and words is hard to separate. Love one, love the other. Some critics—"

But Baines wasn't having any of Basford's slick scholasticisms. He cut him off without a glance and stayed after Kraft. "You did express those sentiments, so widely reported, now didn't you? I mean nobody would say what they didn't mean about something as serious as the love of God, would they?" He was like one of those subtle, ironic police interrogators in the movies. The one who knows the suspect is lying and draws a circle of questions around him to get a final confession.

This was the moment, Kraft thought, to abort all the craziness, to exorcise a lie with another lie. It was the moment to tell them Birdwell had misunderstood his first remarks about the music, about Jesus, that the roller coaster ride ending with the reporter in the station house had begun with a simple misreading. It sounded lame. He might sell it in New York, not here, except that the whole mess would never have happened in New York. Better stick to professionalism.

"Whatever I said or might feel should not affect the program we agreed on. That's all I'm saying."

Baines crushed his cigarette. "Verily thou art neither hot nor cold but lukewarm. Therefore shall I vomit thee out of my mouth!" So much for the separation of personal feelings from public actions. If they were down to New Testament quotations Kraft was in dangerous territory.

But Baines was just getting started. "We have a chance to make a great statement of faith at the same time as putting this school on the map in a big way. That auditorium you conduct in downstairs, the Joe and Josephine Halliburton Hall? I could go to the Halliburton family and get this school enough money to choke a horse if this concert comes off with the right publicity. Enough for all kinds of scholarships, maybe a new building . . ."

The move from the high to the low ground and back was so startling it dizzied Kraft. He couldn't fight on all these fronts at once. Basford moved in. "We're all only concerned with the success of the school, Ben. Surely you see that."

Whipsawed, all Kraft could say was, "Our agreement was that I would choose the programs with the consultation of the board." He could hear that he sounded like a stubborn child. "Consultation is not control."

Baines's mouth turned down in disgust as if he'd seen a low blow, something dishonest.

"You speakin' of your contract? Is that what?"

"Well, I suppose so."

Baines sat down again. Some part of the struggle had shifted, perhaps ended. "I was a lawyer before I ever opened a company of my own and you know what I learned at the New York University Law School?"

Kraft was silent.

"I learned that a contract is only as good as the goodwill behind it."

Threats and counterthreats: a moment for Basford to move in. "Talking about contracts is not what we need. We're discussing a concert program." He wove a comforting web of words . . . the need for personal beliefs to remain personal . . . give Ben a chance to think things over . . . the orchestra waiting for rehearsal downstairs . . .

This time it seemed to work. Baines stood up and took Kraft's hand. He gazed at him with such steady, clear blue eyes. First Maureen, now Baines. Being gazed at like that was like being put in question; not a comfortable feeling. "I wonder

exactly what you did mean to say back there on the highway—
how you feel about it now. Sometimes doubt comes in and
devours faith. The lion does not always lie down with the lamb."

Drowning in a soup of metaphor Kraft mumbled something
about keeping eighty-nine youngsters waiting, retrieved his
hand and fled. He would not wait for the elevator and raced
down the stairs instead, four flights. On the steps he was in a
rage—not at being pushed around at the start of his new job,
not at Basford's slick scholarly manipulations or Jordan Baines's
mixture of Bible and business—a rage at himself, miserable in
his own stubbornness. Who the hell was he, Benjamin Kraft, son
of Lily and Louis Kraft, grandson of Russian Jewish immigrants,
to decide that his own feelings of independence were more
important than the fervor of Art Birdwell, or the longing of
Maureen Kraft, née Donovan, or even the excitement of a
whole alien community about what they took to be a wonderful
confirmation of their faith?

His mind whirls as he whips around landings . . . bits and
pieces . . . at twenty, assistant conductor of the Kansas City Symphony, an intern really, almost no pay and no chance to front
the orchestra, staying in a furnished room rented by the half-
crippled Christian Science landlady Mrs. Gordon who asked if
she might pray for him when he had the flu and he told her to
please not do that, as if he were in the presence of something
eerie, much more superstitious than poor Mrs. Gordon and her
faith which had helped her arthritis so much. . . . Aunt Rose
telling over and over, to anyone who'd listen, the story of the
two-year-old Kraft baby, Joseph, gasping in an oxygen tent on
the verge of giving up his brand new life . . . the rabbi going to
synagogue and changing his name from Joseph to Benjamin so
the Angel of Death, as the story went, wouldn't find little Ben
when he came for him. . . . He'd told the story once to an
amused Koerschner, who'd said, "Ze rabbis think ze angel of

death is zo dumb. If he's zo stupid how come he's still in business after all zese years? Trust me, Benjamin. Superstition will bring you bad luck every time."

He pauses at the ground floor to catch his breath, his thoughts, some composure. He decides to call Art Birdwell that evening. There couldn't be so many Art or Arthur Birdwells in the phone book. But he won't explain—that would be cruel as well as dangerous. No, he will invite him to a concert. Even that might be dangerous, but Kraft felt he had to do something.

He will take an ad in the local newspaper (they only had one) apologizing to the town, to his dear Maureen, for the entire incident; will describe his agnostic background, tell how the music of the Passion had swept him away—claim that the state trooper had misunderstood his explanation. And to back up his decision not to yield, he will invoke his sister Sarah's notions: the anti-Semitism implied in the text of St. John, of St. Matthew. He will take on centuries of theological history in one full-page ad. The ideas are getting loony. His ways out are even more clownish than his way in.

No, there is only one sensible way out: do the St. John. Never mind that it was Baines's blackmail, that he would lose independence and control. He will sing the sublime song of cruelty, suffering and redemption they want from him. The audience of Texas parents and all the others will have a lunatic idea of what the new boy in town is feeling, up there in front of the chorus as they sing *"Herr Unser Herrscher . . .* Lord, our God . . ." There was nothing in the Passion about speeding tickets or lost driver's licenses. But it was apparently too late to change any of that. What started in a rented car with a terrific tape deck could not be stopped—the strange music of that moment had even reached Maureen, unsettling the tricky tightrope walk she'd been doing since they'd met, upsetting the delicate balance he thought they'd arranged for their marriage.

Kraft had little breath left. He leaned against the wall, eyes shut. He saw his grandfather in childhood synagogues each Yom Kippur, rocking back and forth in ancient supplication, caught in a life and piety he obeyed but neither loved nor understood.

THE PLAYERS HAD SCATTERED, sandwiches were being consumed in the front rows of the orchestra, books were being studied yellow markers in hand, onstage four string players took a Schubert quartet apart and attempted to put it back together.

Kraft faked an energy he couldn't feel. "Okay," he called out, clapping his hands. "Sorry for the delay. Places, please." Next to the podium, sitting on Kraft's tall stool, Melanie Rutherford, cellist and librarian, waited patiently.

"Big, boring meeting," Kraft mumbled.

"I haven't put out parts yet. You didn't say—the Bach or the Haydn." She looked at him with a different kind of gaze than he'd been getting that day, from his wife, from Baines. There was no speculation—only a respectful student asking a simple question, waiting for a simple answer.

He took a long breath. "The Haydn," he said. "I'm sorry about the cello solo in the Passion. There'll be other times."

"No problem," she said. "Give me a few minutes." She raced off distributing parts to section leaders as players took their places and resumed the pleasant confusion of warming up.

Kraft opened his own Haydn score and waited, amazed at how easy it was to do what had to be done. Not the right thing, no such thing, just what had to be done. He rotated idly in his chair and saw, from the corner of his eye, that Basford and Baines were sitting in the back row, speaking softly, waiting.

He turned away and faced the stage. Enjoy your life because it respects you, Koerschner had written bewilderingly. Well, perhaps if he performed a Haydn symphony with precision and concern, a simple, secular song, with serious limits to spiritual ambitions; if he forgot for the moment his own grandiose ambitions—not the Maestro, never the Maestro—only the teacher/conductor guiding the Floyd Robbins High School of Performing Arts orchestra, occasional wrong notes and all, maybe then the conundrum would become clear, his life could respect him.

Melanie was back in her seat, her cello at the ready, bow in hand. She nodded. Kraft used no baton. He simply raised a hand and the delicious chaos of tuning and noodling, fragments of scales, concertos, a pop tune glimmering in between, all of it slowly simmered down at last to an apprehensive silence. Then, seized by a bitter need to play a quick trick on Basford, Baines and company, he leaned over towards the young cellist and said, "Melanie, do you know the beginning of 'Es Ist Vollbracht'? It starts with the cello solo."

Embarrassed, she nodded. "Play a little of it for me, the first phrases, would you?" Why not, he thought? Let them think for a minute that they've won. The whole adventure had begun with a trick; let it end with one.

Melanie ruffled some pages, then her cello sang a sweet opening, a descending, dying phrase. Vollbracht meant finished, ended, fulfilled. In the Passion, of course, it meant the completion of all that had been prophesied. The phrase was a lyrical swoon and when she played the D-sharp which began a change of key, she flushed, seemed moved almost to tears. On the other hand, Kraft thought, she might just be embarrassed at suddenly having to play in front of the other students. He did not turn to check a reaction at the rear of the orchestra. His little joke was finished. "Thank you, Melanie," he said. "Well done."

He signaled the concertmaster, who rose and in turn signaled the oboist to sound the A; a scramble of A's and neighboring tones, then quiet.

"Let's get acquainted with the Haydn," Kraft said to the garden of upturned faces. "And with each other. Just a run-through of the first movement."

He was ready to end all arguments, outside and in, ready to begin. Not for him the Bach Passions with their lofty rhetoric, their guilt and expiations. Just a Haydn symphony with its natural gaiety and when it turns sad never quite dark: all in the human scale, as if no one had ever thought of transcendence, as if no one had ever despaired of suffering and loss, as if no young girl had ever nursed a dying twin sister, who took the zip and pizzazz out of her own heart at the same time . . . as if no one had ever been unsatisfied enough, unhappy enough, here to imagine any place else . . . as if no one had ever felt so deep a pain at having to leave this extraordinary earth too soon, this extraordinary earth with its lucky gift of birdsong, its luckier gift of music, this extraordinary earth where, at one time or another, every kind of happiness seems possible.

He did not know in whose name he raised his hands, but he brought them down for the opening chord as firmly as if he did. It rang in the air, it rang inside him; a D major chord, nothing more, nothing less.

Simple. Sufficient. Entirely beautiful.

Duet for Past and Future

Inspired by "The Road Not Taken,"
a poem by Robert Frost

As soon as Reubenfine saw the cello carried out by the tall woman in the quartet, he knew it had to be the Dodd—the one he'd sold to the smooth-talking Frenchman on Fifty-seventh Street. That eighteenth-century English style, that mottled, dark-gleaming varnish, the smallish frame, it had to be the one. It had cost him a lot, giving up that cello; it had taken Alexandra and then Sasha their daughter with it, had landed him in Indianapolis—Indian-noplace he sometimes called it after a few drinks, after work, after getting to know a client well enough to share ironies, even regrets. And now, the cello, if it was the Dodd, had appeared in his exile, a dark, shimmering emblem of things past.

He wondered if BJ, sitting beside him, could sense that he was troubled. She was a smart trick, this particular client; she picked up on everything—a momentary absent tone in his telephone voice might call out a dry comment, "Am I distracting you from something more important?" And right now, there was nothing more important. He was not great at the client-handling game. Some lawyers were; some fried other fish—like spectacular case management, or dramatic court-room stuff. Managing cases and documents was Reubenfine's strong point—not people-pleasing—especially not when advantage was involved. Nevertheless, right now people-pleasing was BJ. A lot hung on the next few days.

She registered his distraction as the quartet onstage discreetly tuned up. Unfolding her program she whispered, "How much for your thoughts right now, Jerry?"

"Not for sale," he said.

"That's going to be news to Stampfer. I thought those thoughts were exactly what I was buying, at a very nice hourly rate." She smiled at him, the smiles growing more sensual in promise as the words grew sharper edges. Stampfer was the senior partner, the rainmaker who owned most of the business.

He'd already told her too much about himself. The extra vodka at dinner and that one glass of wine too many had pushed him a touch too far, laying out across the table his New York music life, his dropping out. But his surprise at seeing what might be his old cello was not the kind of thing he would tell BJ. There was a line he would not cross.

Instead he swerved. "Interesting program," he said.

"Jesus, all Janáček," BJ murmured into her program. "No Schubert, no Beethoven, no Mozart."

"Don't you like a little adventure in your life?" He made a pass at continuing the mild flirting which had run all through dinner at the Pomp and Circumstance Room, the most expensive restaurant in town. He looked directly at her pale blue eyes. She was pretty in a classic Midwestern way: short blonde hair, sweet, childlike rosebud mouth. And out of that innocent-looking mouth came innuendo, sarcasm, sexual promise—all masks for control. She was some number; senior vice president and general counsel, not yet thirty. All the same not his style.

Alexandra had been dark, a biblical beauty. "Your name should have been Esther," he'd told her. "Or maybe Delilah."

"Thanks," she'd said, a dry smile with it; small family jokes. She used to cut his hair; they could always speak in shorthand even in a marriage of only six years.

"Read the program notes," Reubenfine said. "These are the quartets Janáček wrote in his old age for a young love. Don't make that face—you asked for me because you read on my résumé that I'd been a musician."

"I asked for you because it said you were a musician and because you wrote your thesis on Robert Frost and we both went to Columbia."

"Ssshhh."

The quartet began. Reubenfine settled back, prepared to enjoy this. Indianapolis was pretty good on music; the university at Bloomington had a famous music department and that fed the town a little. But Indiana was not first on the major groups' schedule. You didn't get the Juilliard or the Guarneri or the Tokyo too often. Tonight's group, the Montana Quartet, was one of the new all-women ideas. Good reviews, good word of mouth. Reubenfine was up for this. Pretrial preparation had been hell, the trial would be an inferno. This time was his.

The group was smooth, full of energy in the current mode. The first violinist was tiny, older than the others. She handled the virtuoso passages with casual control, but Reubenfine kept his eyes on the cello. Every turn the body of the young cellist took played a different light on the instrument. The A-string sounded sweeter than he recalled, but maybe she played more dolce than Reubenfine ever could. One minute the f-holes looked absolutely familiar, the next he was unsure; the way the endpin held the ground was at once convincing and confusing.

If it was his cello, the upper left side, the part now nestled against the young woman's breasts, was an area where the varnish had been worn away by sweat; only towards the end had he begun to sling a chamois cloth over it before starting to play, as protection. If he could turn that cello around and look, he would know for sure. But as soon as that thought arrived, he realized how foolish it was; whoever had bought his Dodd from Jean-Jacques Grolier, the dealer, could have had the varnish renewed, probably would have. No, the only way was to sit down and hold the instrument between his legs once again. He'd not held one since leaving New York six years ago; his wife, sad but relieved, his seven-year-old daughter tearful, angry.

By the end of the third movement Reubenfine knew what he had to do. A quick plunge backstage after the concert. The conventional congratulations and then he'd tell his story. She would let him examine the instrument—and it would be settled, put to rest. He played his gaze for the first time on the frowning face of the cellist. Not pretty exactly but quite beautiful in a dramatic way, pale skin, bright red slash of lipstick and a passionate style, closing her eyes and opening them unexpectedly as she played; very long, dark hair that spoke her age, maybe twenty-five; full lips, was that what they called a generous mouth, and did that mean she would be generous with the moment, "here, sit down, try it," with a line of people waiting to say nice things about the performance, people waiting to take her to the usual after-concert party? Reubenfine knew the drill. His was an unlikely scenario—but he had no choice. He had to go backstage and settle it.

At intermission the café was a crush but BJ wanted a drink. A tiny table precariously secured, Reubenfine was on his feet, restless. Over his shoulder he tossed, "I have to hit the head. There'll be a line, there always is. Order me an Absolut on the rocks, will you?" She would assume that what he really wanted was a cigarette; the hall was smoke-free.

• • •

THE GREEN ROOM WAS in the usual disarray, open violin cases draped with silk scarves, jackets on chairs, a violin, exposed, on top of the piano in the corner of the room. The cello was hidden in its case, the cellist, too, was invisible. There were only the two violinists and the violist in the room; no visitors at intermission. The first fiddle, the tiny woman with such a formidable technique, came towards the intruder.

"Hello," she said, uncertain.

"Yes," Reubenfine said. He had no prepared speech and now his request would sound foolish, even sinister, coming from a stranger.

"That was beautiful," he said.

"Thank you."

"I was very impressed by the sound of the cello." He paused. The violinist glanced back at the other two women, as if for safety. Then she said, "Eloise will be happy to hear it. She loves that instrument. It's English. I'm afraid she's in the ladies' room."

He listened for the sound of flushing, which might signal an immediate return. All he heard was some kind of distant coughing, a choking sound. Reubenfine glanced at the cello case standing nearby. He was reluctant to let the moment pass. The violinist had no such concern.

"Perhaps you could come back after the concert." She looked at him oddly, he thought, picking up on something in his manner—a little too intense for comfort. A lot of crazies come backstage, Reubenfine remembered from his own days with a quartet. He forced a smile. It was nervy of him to just appear this way but he wasn't nervy enough to ask them to open the case in the absence of its owner.

"Thanks," he said past his false smile. "I'll do that."

• • •

IT SEEMED TO REUBENFINE as if he'd been away for an hour, but it had only been a few minutes, including the few quick drags on a cigarette in the men's room on the way back. The BJ he discovered was comfortable over a Scotch and the ice in his vodka was barely melting. She raised her glass. "Here's to the New York connection."

"You mean us?" He clinked his glass uncertainly against hers.

"I feel connected. It's not just that we're both from New York."

"Then—?"

"We're both masqueraders."

He knew exactly what she meant because he'd told her dangerously too much about that: the sense of acting a part, putting on the lawyer's suit, going to the office, talking "business talk," getting to the crux of things, when part of him remained utterly off-center, concerned with things nonessential. Weather, music, poems—he could brood on significant sunlight or darkening rain, the music he'd heard that morning, or the night before—that was the big soul-difference, how much internal attention he could still give to music so long after giving up the playing. And he read a lot of poetry, Frost and Wallace Stevens, mostly, even some criticism, all of it was poorly isolated in his days, bits and pieces floating into his mind during meetings. It was a kind of lunacy, sharing the twilight, buried life with a client. He should have been talking about the NBA.

"You, a masquerader, BJ? Senior vice president and general counsel."

Her mouth turned down. She chanted: "Two roads diverged in a yellow wood . . ." This was not exactly the woman who made ugly jokes about buying thoughts. Without irony, without the jabbing and probing for weakness, he didn't recognize her. "Don't forget who suggested the concert tonight," she said.

"I think I did."

She laughed and sipped. "Maybe so. But at least I was eager to come. The next few weeks are going to be hard. I figured we needed a soft evening."

"Until you saw it was all Janáček."

"Any man who fell in love past seventy can't be all bad. Face it, Jerry, we're a lot alike. I took a degree in literature before my MBA. You were a musician. We're the new breed in business. Not like Stampfer, hard-nosed, hard-assed. It's them and us. C'mon, admit it. Isn't that the way you think about it?"

"True. But it hadn't occurred to me to include you."

"Include me," she said. Her tone had a directness he'd not heard from her. No spin, no tricks.

His surprise at this spills over and he surprises himself by telling her what he'd promised himself he wouldn't, that he might once have owned the cello of the evening.

"Eighteenth-century English. Dodd. He also made elegant bows with ivory frogs, unusual."

"Can you tell from such a distance?" she asks, a lawyer-question.

"I don't know. I could be imagining it. That cello had so much baggage with it. It was a wedding present from my wife."

He's carried that baggage alone for so long that he somehow slips into sharing the weight of it. He tells her about the slow disillusionment with the musical life, his delight at lucking out by landing in a new quartet, with a manager and a tour all set up, delight becoming a casualty after the quartet folded, the wrong programs, the wrong bookings, maybe the wrong manager, who finally dropped them.

By this time little Sasha was ready for private school, the public ones where they lived were dark options and Sasha so bright. Reubenfine was back to putting together a living, jobbing around New York, a theater gig, a ballet orchestra, recording television shows, whatever came up.

What his would-be pianist mother had always called his musical destiny had become just a way to make a living. He was bitter and Alexandra was bitter at his bitterness. Finally, he'd sold the Dodd, wedding present or not, to finance law school and she'd taken it as a betrayal. All that time of doing without, in exchange for high musical hopes, all that dwindling down to law school, all that feeling like people especially blessed by music who could bless others with their playing—all that boiling down to a résumé and a lot of phone calls.

Of course, by that time they weren't talking the same language anymore. The lawyer glut hit and when it turned out the only job offer was from Stampfer and Partners in Indianapolis, everyone was relieved, everyone except Sasha, who wouldn't even kiss him good-bye. Alexandra couldn't leave New York because she had a thirteen-week gig accompanying a singer. By the time it arrived, the divorce was only a coda.

BJ was finishing her second Scotch but she listened, nodding soberly. "It's the road not taken," she said, "like the Frost poem. The guy in the poem took the road less traveled by. You left it," she said. "I mean how many full-time musicians are there in America? You chose a road cluttered with lawyers and clients, briefs, discovery of documents. Does it give you delight—that was your word, wasn't it, about playing quartets?"

"A lot of lawyers take pleasure in what they do."

"We're not talking about a lot of lawyers. This is you and me, Jerry Reubenfine and BJ Camden."

"Well," he said. "What *about* BJ Camden?"

The tables around them were clearing out. The first warning bell had sounded. This oddest of intermissions was coming to a close. Behind them, the bartender was clearing off glasses and soggy napkins and emptying coins and bills from a glass.

BJ spread a wan smile above her drink.

"Oh, her," she said. "Beryl Camden."

"Is that who BJ is?"

"Used to be," she said and twisted in her chair looking for a waiter.

"They'll be starting soon," he said.

But the bartender had seen her signal. Another round appeared. BJ was on a personal jag. He'd been working with her for three months but he'd never seen her so open, so pushed to tell.

She said, "My road is full of hairpin turns and speeding BMWs—heavy traffic. I've made all kinds of choices about men, about jobs, not sure about any of them."

"Is that why you come on so strong, sometimes?"

"May be," she said. "Even this dumb idea of being called BJ. My name is Beryl Jane but I use BJ to help make a place for me in a tough world. It's the kind of thing you do when you're not quite sure about who you are or who you're supposed to be. Probably why I let myself drink just a little too much every night. Extra imported confidence." She started on the new Scotch. They had the café to themselves. It was like a date or a pickup in a movie, with music beginning in the background.

Applause filtered in. In the corner above the bar a TV monitor mirrored the stage. The quartet was back, the cellist adjusting the length of her endpin while the others softly tuned. Eloise, the fiddler had called her backstage. She didn't look like an Eloise, too dark in color and expression.

He pushed his chair back. "They're starting," he said. "We'd better go."

"For Christ's sake, it's just another piece by the same composer. You can listen in here. Let's talk."

Reubenfine was apprehensive. He'd already told her too much. The cello wasn't his alone anymore; she knew about it and what notes it had played in his song. He had to get out. Tomorrow's meeting would be tricky, but right now the trick was to get through the evening. From the TV and the hall behind them came a shaky kind of indistinct stereo sound. The next Janáček quartet, lyric and dissonant.

"In fact," BJ says, "I'm talked out and listened out. Let's just go. Back to my place."

"I can't," he says. "I'm bugged about that cello. I've got to find out. I'll go backstage after they're finished. See if she'll give me a closer look."

"What's the difference? You chose the road more traveled by—and the cello paid for it.

"I paid for it," Reubenfine says. "I think I still am."

BJ stands up quickly and throws some bills down on the check, without looking, the way people do in old movies on TV. Reubenfine pushes his chair back and kisses her lightly on the cheek, knowing he might be kissing a lot of hard-earned gains good-bye. He knows he is being perverse—that the glimpse of what might be his cello has turned his head sour, made him a touch crazy in regard to present practicalities—a kamikaze mood.

REUBENFINE STOOD BEHIND THE last row waiting for the end, ready to race, planning to be the first one backstage, anxious for a clear shot. But there was enough enthusiasm from the audience for an encore. The first violin announced it: the slow movement from Schubert's *Death and the Maiden.* Listening to the opening chords he knew well, remembering the times he'd played them, he felt the vodka hit, dizzying.

His teacher, old Mrs. Rosanoff, had told him he had an instinct for the song hidden in the notes. "The composer hides the song," she said, large and in command of truth, surrounded by yards of black silk and lace. "The notes are a code. Just knowing how to break the code is the surface. You, my boy, have the sense of the hidden song. On the other hand, you are frequently out of tune on the upper A-string. Beware!" Like all gods Mrs. Rosanoff giveth and Mrs. Rosanoff taketh away in the same sentence.

Reubenfine was quite drunk, afloat in memory and apprehension. The instant the last note floated to rest he was on his way.

"THAT'S HIM," THE VIOLINIST murmured when Reubenfine entered. The cellist, Eloise, was wiping resin dust from the cello with a tan chamois cloth preparatory to putting it to rest in its case. It was that last moment of privacy before the trickle of visitors carrying congratulations. Reubenfine quickly filled in the blanks—the fiddler had apparently told Eloise that some weirdo had come back at intermission, babbling about her cello while she was in the john.

He moved right next to her, sensing he was standing too close for politeness, but the polite moment had passed.

"I think I recognize that cello. Where did you buy it?"

It was the wrong opener, he would have grabbed the words and choked on them if he could. He should have told her how beautifully she'd played the solo in the Schubert, remarked about the clarity of her tone on the A-string.

"I bought it from a collector in Phoenix," she said. She did not look at him.

"It's a Dodd, isn't it?"

She nodded. People were starting to form a line in the doorway.

It was now or never. "May I see it." And instead of just looking closer he brushed past her, jostled her and tried to grasp the neck of the instrument. He could see himself behaving like a drunk in the movies but he couldn't stop. She took a step backwards, still holding tightly to the cello. He got a blur of her perfume, something light and lilac.

She straightened up and stared at Reubenfine. He never noticed the color of people's eyes but hers were a startling blue, unclouded. "Don't," she said. "It's not stolen or anything. I have all the papers from Hill in London." She grabbed it firmly, lowered the endpin and opened the hard case, standing next to her, a silent witness.

The petite fiddler came over to them. "Eloise," she said. "Are you okay? Your father and his friend are here."

"She's fine," Reubenfine said, backing towards the doorway. "I was just going."

As he left he caught one last look at the Dodd before it disappeared into the case. It was probably not his; it seemed more elegant, the varnish was lighter, the curve of the f-holes more shapely.

ON THE STEPS OF the hall Reubenfine stood alone, smoking a cigarette while around him the last of the audience headed for the safety of their cars. The young cellist came out carrying her case in a sling over her shoulder. Seeing her outside, wearing a spring coat and a white wool scarf, he saw she couldn't be more than twenty-five, if that. During the concert, her black hair had been in her eyes, around her shoulders, wisps in her lips to be spat out while turning a page. Now it was drawn into a tight ponytail, still long, still a reminder of her youth. Afraid for her to notice him, embarrassed, Reubenfine half turned away, waiting for her to move on. But she looked around and stopped cold.

"Shit," she said. They were the only people on the steps and he said, "Excuse me?"

"My gang left. I told them it was okay, like an idiot. Now there are no cabs."

"I'll give you a lift."

She looked past him and then below his eyes, her turn to be embarrassed. "No, I'll call for a cab."

"It's late. I'll drop you. Give me a chance to make up for my bad manners back there."

She shook her head but it struck Reubenfine as a tentative gesture. "I'll take a cigarette, though, if you can spare one. I'm trying to quit." He lit it for her in the chilly evening air. Spring came late in Indiana and the nights were often cold. She joined a breath of smoke to the night air and said, "I was the one who was rude. I got flustered. I wasn't sure what was up with you."

"You've got it in reverse," Reubenfine said. "Guy comes backstage, maybe a little vodka on his breath, sort of grabs at you and your cello. What are you supposed to do, put out the welcome mat?"

For the first time her gaze settled directly at Reubenfine, meeting his own. He had the sudden, crazy sense that something in her had liked the way he'd pushed at her to get a look, the heedlessness, the shoving.

"Alphonse and Gaston," she said. "Trying for the rude-of-the-night award." She dragged in a breath of smoke and blew out rings, the way grown-ups used to do to entertain children. She smiled. "Here we are," she said. "The last two smokers in America." There was something sullen about her low-lidded eyes and her swollen lips, daring the world to push her and see what happened.

LATER, SITTING UP IN bed, she held the sheet over her small breasts, oddly shy, as if she knew him well enough to make love in her hotel room after a half-hour acquaintance over a cello, but not well enough for casual nakedness. "You know," she said, "I was throwing up, before, when you came back at intermission."

"I thought I heard kind of funny sounds coming from the bathroom." He pulled himself up on one elbow to face her. "Are you pregnant?"

"No, just miserable."

"Can I know why?"

"You can't tell miseries so quickly. I can tell you a happiness, though." She turned and drowned him in the black hair she'd taken down before falling back onto the big bed in the little room. "What we just did, that was a happiness."

"But I told you God knows whatall awful stuff about myself, in the car."

He had, in fact, giddy with vodka and anxiety, poured out a lot of his sense of being stranded, not quite rid of an old Jerry Reubenfine, not quite comfortable with any new one; how he'd refused to hold a cello in his arms again, he was a lawyer now, a businessman, and you couldn't mix life-metaphors or you'd drive yourself crazy with regret and longing. He left out about the Dodd, not quite knowing why, surprised at how ready he was to lay all this stuff out to a stranger. Even down to the half-furnished apartment—a transient but going nowhere else. All in a ten-minute drive. Now it was her turn.

Eloise was turning away from him suddenly, a little weepy.

"Hey," he said, trying to pull her back down on the pillow but now she had a shoulder of iron.

"I was throwing up, I always throw up on concert nights because I hate the life, my life . . ." She turned back towards him. "You did the right thing, you got out. You can play for yourself, for your own joy—"

"But I don't," he said. "Not once since I quit, since New York." But she barreled on, not listening.

"You can't imagine how rotten it is, the confusion, the competition—the lousy money; after a while you're practicing the Bach suites or the Dvorak concerto and you wonder why—it doesn't have a damned thing to do with anything—you don't want an orchestra job because that's so fucking boring and a solo career is out because you need money behind you—and I might not be all that good, and the quartet seems more solid except when the reviews say you're good but not as good as the Guarneri or the Emerson. My mother warned me about getting into it—she used to play viola in the symphony here but I was so pissed at her about the divorce and marrying this rich guy with a slew of fishing boats and going to live in the Bahamas that I didn't listen—so I quit school and got myself into this music life and the only fun I have is maybe picking up a groupie on the road. You didn't know there were chamber music groupies? I thought maybe you were one of them, at first."

A wave of blood flushed her face and she took a breath. Reubenfine saw his moment. "Are you done?" he said.

"No," she said.

"Yes," he said.

He was furious. She had seemed so passionately poised above her cello, above the upturned faces of the listening audience. Watching her, listening to her confident playing of Janáček on that lyric cello, Reubenfine had been certain that she had the answer, that she was the answer. Had *no one* ever taken the right road? More traveled by, less traveled by, who gave a shit! Everyone nursing their maybes; everyone, everywhere, secretly throwing up in disgust at the path they were on, longing for some other direction inscribed on some invisible, unavailable map.

Reubenfine jerks the sheet from her hands and pushes her down onto the nest of tangled linen and pillows. This is an angry way to do it, grabbing at her breasts, rushing her legs apart, angry, a little rough. Isn't this what she bargained for, he thinks, taking up with a stranger who jostles her backstage? And she does respond, making different sounds than before, her eyes shutting, then opening, excited. It brings him less pleasure than the easy, surprising way they'd first fallen into bed, but he is serving other pressures than plain pleasure. To keep some sense of play in it he rolls her over on top of him. The flood of black hair that had covered the cello now covers him. Over her shoulder, past the troubling curve of her sweet cheek, he sees the cello case looming large, patient.

Afterwards, she was calmer, reaching for a cigarette and her lighter.

"Hey," he said, "you can't smoke in bed."

"I can do anything I want in bed," she said, going into her smoke circles number again.

"My God, how old are you?"

She scowled as if she'd been asked to show her ID at a bar.

"Twenty-five," she said. "But a tired twenty-five. How old are you?"

"Thirty-six," he said. "At twenty-five I was never tired."

She blew a sassy ring at him.

Reubenfine laughed, not quite sure why. "Where'd you learn to do that?"

"My father. Professor Schuler taught me everything I know."

"Professor of what?"

"Chinese Literature—at the university here. He came back-stage tonight with his latest girlfriend."

She was bitter about the girlfriend, a student poet about Eloise's age. "It's the old graduate student–professor joke." Only she didn't find it amusing. They were shacked up now and even though the Quartet's tour was ending back home where it started Eloise didn't want to live at home. She didn't want to be having breakfast with the latest poet in her father's life while he taught an early class. Hence, a hotel room in her hometown.

"Listen," Reubenfine said. "You can't live in a hotel forever. Must cost a fortune."

There was, it turned out, a piano trio leaving for a six-week Midwest tour. The cellist was sick and Eloise would have to rehearse the Archduke, the two Mendelssohns and the Shostakovich in a week and then take off.

"I'm not sure I want to do it," she said.

"Why not?"

She rolled out of bed and hopped towards the bathroom. The sheet-veil was forgotten. Quite sober, now, Reubenfine used his eyes the way he'd used his hands and mouth a short while before—grazing long legs, young breasts that moved with, not against, the rest of her body; skin the shade of eggshells. He saw, now, a Rorschach-shaped wine stain starting just under her rib cage, extending down to the center of her stomach.

The startling imperfection against the perfect white skin moved him, oddly. She was so beautifully formed and this stain was so shapeless, so harshly shaded. Perhaps it was not her breasts she'd been shyly hiding when she'd kept the sheet between them for so long.

Eloise chose to ignore where his gaze might have landed. She stuck with her theme. "Haven't you been listening, Mister Rubenstein?"

"Reuben*fine!*" He laughed at how new they were to each other.

"Well, I'm the same as you. I'm not sure I'm right or wrong, lost or found. Don't talk to me until you've done twenty-five one-nighters in a month, playing for strangers, talking to strangers, most of whom don't know a damn thing about what they're listening to."

She opened the bathroom door. "For God's sake, you think you're the only one in the world who can't stand that what they do isn't who they are?" She vanished into the bathroom and Reubenfine listened anxiously. If she started her vomiting routine he wasn't sure how he would handle it. Happily, the air carried first tap water and then flushing sounds.

Reubenfine was half-dozing when she got back into bed.

He said, "Did you really think I was one of your groupies?"

She nodded. "I figured that stuff about the cello was a gag, just a way to get close and start something."

"You're a wild thing, aren't you?"

"Why, because I'm in bed with you so quick? The year of the divorce I fucked every guy I knew and a few I didn't. I suppose that makes me a wild thing."

"But it doesn't make me one of your groupies. I was completely straight about the cello. The minute you walked out on that stage holding the Dodd out in front of you—"

And he told her how sure he'd been that it was the instrument, the wedding present from Alexandra, a ticket to truth, beauty and success. When truth finally became the ugly truth and Jean-Jacques Grolier entered the picture with an offer—

"How long ago was this?" She was into it now, absently wiping perspiration from her forehead with a corner of the sheet.

"About six years ago."

Absorbed now, she took the lead, told him stories about cellos she's played and the journeys they have made from sets of hands to other sets of hands, from one life to a completely different life—a Montagnana sold by the estate of a German car dealer for peanuts, bought by a stock broker–amateur player then sold as part of a divorce settlement—a Guarnerius that had been carried by a family fleeing the Russian Revolution, finding safety in Harbin on the Chinese border, bringing it to New York where they sold it to a collector who donated it as a tax deduction to his alma mater, the University of Indiana at Bloomington, where it was loaned to Eloise Schuler's teacher as part of his employment contract. She had found it thrilling to touch, to play the instrument made in Cremona, in Italy, centuries ago, carried in refuge from the Russian Revolution and finally under her fingers in prosaic Indiana.

Weaving these threads into stories she was now quite different, more of a youngster, innocent of anger or ennui, fascinated by the romance of musical instruments and their destinies. She gave this as much energy as she had given to her passionate litany of disappointments.

"It's like the *Thousand and One Nights,*" she said. "Go take it out and see if it's yours. Go on."

He hesitated. "Ah, well," he said. "It's yours now." She pushed him, then wrestled, giggling, the bedclothes falling away from them. Then, suddenly, Eloise leaned over him and surprised them both touching her mouth lightly to his—the first time not connected to sex. "Try it out," she said. "See what you think."

He removed the instrument from its case thinking how funny the scene might seem, the three of them naked now, vulnerable: he, Eloise and the cello in his hands. It would have been a small thing to twirl it and check the upper back where the varnish would have been worn away by years of sweaty playing—the only professional cellist in the world not to use a protective cloth; careless, heedless of all things precious. Even if someone had revarnished it, you could usually tell the new from the old all around it. But he did not.

He sat down, the leather chair chilly under his buttocks, the wood of the cello's back touching his limp penis, the bow in hand, looking down at the length of the fingerboard, the strings. It was the old, familiar position of years, the repeated first moment of a lifetime, the moment before making music. A fine mist of resin dust sprinkled on the fingerboard, on the lower curve of the cello, around the f-holes.

"Well," she said. "Is it the one, was it yours?"

He looked at her across the curve of the cello. He could tell they were not finished, might never be finished with each other. But perhaps they would only continue this naked duet for a few more weeks until it grew too heavy to continue and they would drop it and she would move on, back to her unsatisfactory, edgy, complaining life: the wrong music, wrong cities, the wrong lovers. Or maybe she would stay here with him, rehearse a life together, find local string players, pianists, play chamber music of every numerical count: duets, trios, quartets, quintets, sextets—an almost infinite choice; would play, as she had put it miserably, for their own joy.

New, more complicated friends would show up, drawn by the double life on display—legal/musical; people who would admire the oxymoron of such an arrangement. They would have a circle. She would transform Indian-noplace into a genuine place; he could stop being a visitor in his own life. She'd spoken of giving up smoking—they would both give up smoking! He would calm her down, mute the wildness, and she would lend him energy, confidence—he would learn to handle clients like BJ without confrontation, without having to win or lose.

She was so young, bitter. If he could sweeten that bitterness, maybe children, one, two, who could know? Reubenfine thought ahead, imagining even more possibilities—a teenaged Sasha visiting an infant half sister or brother, instead of contributing anger, resentment, she would enjoy Eloise, she would imitate her rough-and-tumble style; the rift of divorce and distance might be healed. From an irritable chance encounter to a life. It was at least possible.

Hypnotized, provoked by his long silence behind the cello, Eloise sat up. The sheet fell again to her flat stomach and she leaned towards him, open, unguarded. The long sadness of the wine stain below her breasts spreading on her stomach gleamed in the light.

"Well," she said, eager as a child to hear the end of a story, "what do you think? Is it true? Was it ever yours?"

He began to play, choosing at random the opening of the Bach G major unaccompanied suite. Hardly registering how well he could still play, Reubenfine stared blindly at the naked young woman in the hotel bed, stared at what seemed to him his astonishingly good fortune.

"I don't know," he said. "I don't care."

A Philosopher's Honeymoon

Inspired by "The Man on the Dump,"
a poem by Wallace Stevens

Abrams, a rabbi on the run, woke to an awful confluence of smells. Along with the ripe, rank odors of garbage and the coppery smell of rust there were rotting flowers, sweet to his exhausted nose for all of that. There was something soft moving under him giving off an odor he could not place, seaweed, potato peelings, an old couch; something he could only hope was still alive; not that there was any reason to assume he'd fallen asleep close to something dead the night before, more like morning when he'd hit the sack, dead drunk at the end on some sweet liqueur, how could he be expected to know what he'd lain on. This was a new low in sacking out, the dump just outside the town limits, Abrams just barely inside his own limits: of drink, of loss, hope, fatigue.

He groped under his legs and felt—legs, small, bony, fur. A quick look and he saw it was a dog. Dear God, he said out of anxiety, out of habit, a little out of irony, not Adonay, not Elohim, just Dear God—don't let it be dead. Don't let me have spent the night and part of the day sleeping with a dead dog. He was not even certain why it would be so much more humiliating to have lain with a dead dog than a live one. Either was a far cry from percale sheets, white or patterned, a far cry from Beth Abrams's perfectly patterned life and home on Water Street, full of elegant touches because she had instinctive taste, but not pretentious, everything in scale, books the center of gravity, the house, like the life, clean, tasteful, inexpensive by necessity: the quintessential rabbi's home. And why not? Beth meant house in Hebrew, his home was Beth Abrams, his temple was Beth Shalom, house of peace.

The dog, who essentially had been lying with Abrams, not beneath him, wobbled to his feet, shook himself weakly and wandered towards a huddle of people cooking something in a large can over an improvised fire. What brought a dog to this lousy end, this place, Abrams wondered, not pursuing it further in thought, what, after all, could bring anybody here?

He stretched his bony legs. He'd lost a fair amount of weight since hitting the road or the skids, whatever it was he'd hit that had landed him here, skinnier but still going, on the dump. He stood up, leaning on an automobile tire for leverage. He stared at the tire; it had the gray, anonymous coloring of discarded parts, of alien animal skin. Abrams didn't care for the thought; all too easy to think of himself as a discarded part, as an alien animal these days.

Oh, bullshit! He'd wanted to surprise his self-pity, get rid of it. Instead, he surprised himself by speaking the word aloud. Careful, he thought. Bad enough being on the dump. Once you start being one of those people you see talking to themselves— he shook his head, a cautionary, rabbinic movement. It was a mistake. His head reminded him about pain; his new life, a headache without a medicine cabinet full of aspirin, ibuprofen, Tylenol, Valium. He doubted that any of his willy-nilly companions consoling themselves, a few yards away, with something hot, would be able to offer an aspirin let alone any more exotic nostrums for his ache.

At his feet were strewn a smattering of objects he'd shared his bed with. A clump of yellow flowers wrapped in newspaper held his gaze, azaleas they were, he could tell because Beth's sister, Rowena, had brought them azaleas and had lectured him, as she lectured everyone, about their care and feeding; Rowena, who had, at the end, turned out to be one of his worst mistakes.

Abrams's mouth was dry yet he felt a desperate need to spit—as if by spitting he could clear his mouth of the mixture of foul tastes, could purify something, at least his miserable, sour breath. He spat into the dust, someplace clear, wanting to spare the azaleas, to spare the scatter of books, mostly paperbacks, sprawling next to where he'd slept, sharing a bed of gravel and ash. God, who would send books to the dump. Books were meant to go from hand to hand, eye to eye, forever, or as long as their bindings held pages together. Abrams knelt and browsed, old habits die hard even on the dump.

A Complete Guide to the Automobile and Its Parts . . . Forever Amber . . . The Great War and Modern Memory. . . . He didn't need a book at the moment. Abrams had brought his book with him, only one book in his flight, stuffed into his jacket pocket. *The Palm at the End of the Mind: Poems by Wallace Stevens.* He pulled it out and rifled the pages, tempted to add it to the collection in the dirt.

On impulse he did it—tossed it into the filthy, torn collection at his feet. It was the book with which he'd antagonized the Women's Reading Circle at his temple, suggesting that they introduce poetry into their list—a needed change from Chaim Potok, from Leo Rosten and *The Joys of Yiddish.* They'd nervously agreed but had thought perhaps of Longfellow, of Edna St. Vincent Millay, then in comes Stevens with his *Notes towards a*

Supreme Fiction, his difficult images, his philosophical references. He'd tried to make it less painful with "Postcard from a Volcano," an easier job, but it was a bad number from the start, the women made to feel foolish, inadequate, the opposite of what he'd had in mind. He'd already been told that some in the congregation were not happy with him using so many references to T. S. Eliot, to Auden and even more obscure poets in his sermons. Don't think just because we're Reform—and so on. That might go down in New York at Temple Emanu-El, they said, not here in Hillcrest.

Yet another misstep from Abrams, pretentious, insensitive, according to Beth; trying to make people into what they weren't, instead of meeting them on their own ground— another melody added to their old sweet song of bedtime discord. Useless to tell her again how moving the poems were to him, how consoling in a difficult life, so once again he shut up, sulked, drank. And when he'd started his buried life, the secretive attempt to write stories based on poems that moved him, he'd said nothing to Beth.

Abrams bent and retrieved the Stevens. Why had he grabbed it out of all the possible books for a fugitive journey whose end was dim, obscure? As a reminder of his humiliating failure with the Women's Reading Circle? Or because the poems could be read and read again with talmudic persistence, giving a different pleasure each time? Both! An action overdetermined like actions in Freud's dreams.

Abrams brushed dirt and fragments of gravel from the book. The book was damp and he wasn't too happy about what the yellowish stains might represent—he'd slept on the ground more than once, his jacket rolled up as portable pillow, had sometimes peed haphazardly. But the pages turned and were readable and he stuck it back into his jacket. He was thus reminded that he had to pee now, but where? Even here modesty made its claim. There were rusted remains of a car a few yards west, the dropping sun behind it, but it looked too low to offer privacy. Closer in was a tree. Gnarled, almost bare as if to spite the spring season, it was like a tree in a Beckett play. It would serve.

Afterwards, he walked towards the trio thinking how lucky for all of them that it was a hazy, warm spring day. The fire was for some kind of food, not warmth. Day? The day was fading. The air had a bluish tinge, the sky would be making a change towards evening soon. How long had he slept—maybe a night and two-thirds of a day. His watch was gone, he had no idea where. His worst toot yet.

The presence of the woman surprised Abrams. He was old-fashioned enough to have always suffered a special frisson of horror whenever he'd seen a woman in the street, on the skids. And here, of all places in the good green world. She was pretty, still young though it was hard to be sure about that, her reddish hair any which way, skin cracked around the mouth, no lipstick, at least not lately. The man next to her was large, he needed a lot of space, even his head was grand. Beside him was a delicate, trembling sort of man, quite old judging by the gray, by the shuffling gait as he rose to poke at the fire.

They made room for Abrams as naturally as if he'd been expected. He came right to the point.

"What's in the can?"

"Soup," the woman said. "Soup du jour."

"The jour is almost over," the large man said, admiration in his voice. "Mary Louise cheers us up with a little French talk now and then."

Mary Louise handed Abrams a Campbell's soup can. She used a cardboard cup to transfer soup from the large can over the fire to the small one in Abrams's hand. It took a long time. It tasted like tomato-flavored water decorated with pepper. By the time he drank the cupful it felt as if he'd been sitting there for a long time and these were people he knew. He thought, and had thought before in his pre-dump life, about how quickly a rabbi gets to be comfortable with strangers—like his professional siblings, analysts, therapists of all stripes, priests, visible reminders of the strangeness of everyone.

Knowing people's names usually helped and he said, speaking to the fire and thus to all three, "I'm Jack Abrams." Usually followed with "Rabbi of Temple Beth Shalom," but at this moment it seemed more sensible to say, "Thanks for the soup."

Nobody replied to this. A flutter of birds pouring an awful racket from their beaks and coming too close to the small circle around the fire made the old man scramble and wave his arms at them.

"Take it easy Eddy," Mary Louise said.

"Damned birds," Eddy muttered and subsided. "Godawful noise."

"What kind of birds are they?" Abrams asked and felt awkward at once. Ornithology could not be a great concern on the dump. But Mary Louise surprised him. "Grackles," she said. "These here are grackles. A bird of the South. Quarrelsome sort."

"Like crows," Abrams offered.

"Sort of."

"Mary Louise knows all hell about things," the large man said.

"Oh please Rory. Lay off."

Rory addressed Abrams directly. "It's one of the reasons I'm in love with her."

"Jesus!" Mary Louise looked to Abrams as if for rescue. Her eyelids were either oddly shaded or she carried the remnants of eyeshadow, purplish in the darkening air. "Even here, he carries on. Can you believe it?"

Abrams smiled. He was more comfortable with this moment, was used to a life of generalized discourse. Words he could handle, however obliquely attached to lives and places.

"Yes," he said. "Love happens anywhere, everywhere."

Rory nodded his almost hydrocephalic head in sage agreement. But in the few seconds which passed, Abrams's own words tasted foolish in his mouth, dumb echoes—years of automatic rabbinic response. He would have to stay away from opinions, especially banal, rhetorical ones, trapdoors waiting to send him spinning into a pit of self-disgust.

He remembered the retiring Rabbi Greenwald at Beth Shalom, replaced by Abrams eight years ago. The older man had moved from the residence supplied by the congregation, had taken a house on the not-so-fancy part of Lake Shore Drive, and a joke went around:

Question: Does Greenwald have a view of the lake?

Answer: Honey, he's a rabbi, he has an opinion on everything.

Instead of cheering him, the remembered moment of self-mocking malice triggered gloom. Or had it been the word love spoken here on the dump? He'd loved Beth, had even been in love. But that hadn't prevented his whole enterprise from going south. Years of his uncertainty, his endless retracing of his footsteps, a man always in question, had turned her from a witty charmer into a scold.

Love, that solemn, sacred word so beloved of songwriters and clergymen, hadn't helped him believe in his vocation, hadn't made him a good teacher—that was all a rabbi was, a teacher, in spite of all the fancy, ancient reverberations of the word; love hadn't granted him the secret of being a good husband, hadn't resolved the dilemma of children refusing to arrive after years of making love, at first with passionate hope, later with cheerless persistence. How could you make love, anyway? An odd phrase, peculiar term of manufacture. Only a God could do that and if he existed he didn't do it often or well enough.

"Lukewarm! You'll be thinking about what to do with your life when you're seventy. For Christ's sake be a rabbi or don't— but be something. Don't be a rabbi with a half-finished novel, a bunch of poems and afraid to adopt a child because it's the last nail in the coffin of having your own kids. Jesus!" He made no mention of the incongruity of Beth's eternal use of Christian imagery in her expletives. She was always a volatile woman; he'd liked that in her in the beginning. His was a more quiet soul, a quiet style. She needed more opposition, more sparks with which to ignite her flame.

They must be going crazy at Temple Beth Shalom. . . . He'd not told anybody anything—just vanished. A nasty, cruel thing to do, given all the responsibilities—but it was all he could manage. By now the police will have come up empty and a period of mourning will have begun.

The old man, Eddy, was still standing at the perimeter of the makeshift fire, as if on guard against the return of the grackles. Mary Louise was filling a container with soup and handing it to an adoring Rory. Suddenly Abrams could not sit there one minute more, did not want to hear another word about dump-love. He would have liked a drink but he had no bottle, no glass available to him, not a dollar left in his pocket. He took the book of poems from his jacket pocket and walked away from the group.

Mary Louise looked over at Abrams and said, "What'd you used to do, Mister—I mean before you stumbled?"

"She calls our troubles stumbling," Rory said, marveling. "Isn't she something?"

Abrams paused, wondering how to reply, then from a life-time of habit came the truth. "I was a rabbi," he said, surprised at his use of the past tense, as if this was the famed life after death, damned souls introducing themselves, instead of just the worst morning after, in months of mornings after. He kept walking, wanting no more discourse, no more exchange of information. "Thanks for the soup," he called out.

Abrams retreated to the tree behind which he'd pissed and sat down on the other side of it. He was waiting until he felt the strength to get up and out, to go home, apologize to Beth, explain to the board of directors, check into Hillcrest Hospital, call an end to his loony flight; or maybe to call Rowena and dry out at her apartment, he remembered how deliciously deep her bathtub was, and he would soak himself clean and ask her not to call her sister until he was ready, which might be never.

To distract himself, to stall, he rambled through the book of poems. Reading had been his irreproachable vice; in childhood he read to escape his foolish, all too often unemployed, father, his ailing mother, later he read to put off responsibilities. It was better than drinking. He leafed past the ones he knew—"Post-card from a Volcano," "The Snowman," until he skimmed past page 94 and saw the title "The Man on the Dump."

It was like a moment in a dream, the moment in which everything points with portents and signs to some meaning you can feel but not understand, least of all after you've woken up. His skin was shuddery while he read, an eerie sensation, but his headache was gone.

> Day creeps down. The moon is creeping up.
> The sun is a corbeil of flowers the moon Blanche
> Places there, a bouquet. Ho-ho . . . The dump is full
> Of images. Days pass like papers from a press.

Abrams, of course, knew the poem well. Jerry Cardoza, his obsessive roommate at Amherst, had done a major paper on

it, had kept Abrams up with his endless interpretations and rein-
terpretations so that, finally, an exhausted Abrams felt like he'd
written the poem himself, would never forget it. It was Cardoza
who'd started him on Stevens. Later, when Abrams was at the
seminary, he'd amused himself by counting the number of
times the word *rabbi* appeared in the poems by a New England
gentile. More than thirty, as he recalled.

Reading was almost the same as remembering and Abrams
laughed aloud, remembering something about last night. He'd
left the Scat Bar, deafened by the million decibels of the rap
music jukebox where the triumphant Hispanic guy in the wide,
brilliant red suspenders had been buying the drinks; had
walked past the railroad tracks, had seen what seemed at first to
be simply a graveyard for old, rusted automobile parts but which
turned out to be nothing less than a dump, perhaps the town
dump. He wasn't even sure which town he was in, but he
thought it might be Larkspur, only a few miles from his home in
Hillcrest.

Giggling to himself, beat, teary with self-pity, Abrams had
thought "why not?", remembering "The Man on the Dump," the
pimply, driven Cardoza and his A paper, both of them nineteen,
and remembered all the hopes and confusions of the time of
Amherst. What the hell, he'd thought, if you could call such
dizzy, sodden fragments thought, go ahead, act it out, do it, be it,
don't just read and talk and drink, be something, if only the rock
bottom. That was sort of the way it had gone and he'd lain down
in the dark next to something soft, something large, and slept.

Now, that night gone and most of the next day, Abrams
skated on the surface of the poem, a better description than
reading because the piece was complicated and he was hearing
in his jumbled mind both the images on the page and the endless conversations with Cardoza, intent on getting his Ph.D. and
setting the academic world on fire.

> . . . The dump is full
> Of images. Days pass like papers from a press. . . .

Then a bunch of what Stevens calls janitor's poems of every day which show up at the dump:

> . . . the wrapper on the can of pears,
> the cat in the paper-bag, the corset, the box
> From Esthonia: the tiger chest for tea.

Abrams could now have added the piss-yellow paperbacks. But none of this carried the main impression he recalled from the poem, the sense of a tiredness, of a distaste for used things . . . well, yes, maybe used things was more like it . . .

> The freshness of night has been fresh a long time,
> The freshness of morning . . .

How could freshness be fresh for a long time? Didn't that imply staleness? And then came a passage about dew. As a city boy in summer camp he'd wondered about the evening dew. He'd expected morning dew. But why the evening, too?

> . . . the dew in the green
> Smacks like fresh water in a can, like the sea
> On a coconut—how many men have copied dew
> For buttons, how many women have covered themselves
> With dew, dew dresses, stones and chains of dew, heads
> Of the floweriest flowers dewed with the dewiest dew . . .

Mocking the nice, fresh dew, of course . . . copied a key word here . . . as tired of the conventional dew in poetry, in people's minds, as Gertrude Stein was tired of the red, red rose. It was with such ideas that Cardoza had lectured him with passion—a passion on behalf of a poet tired of used things, fed up with living on the dump of old, received images.

Abrams's heart jumped in him, it was like being young again. Cardoza pacing the room, spewing lines, images and interpretations; Abrams, uncertain of his future: a writer, a teacher, a rabbi—his father's goal for him—mostly eager to read, write, get laid. In this vulnerable state, Cardoza had had him dazzled, confused, hypnotized.

He'd died still young, poor Cardoza, long after they'd lost track of each other; the circumstances suggested suicide, but when Abrams called Cardoza's father he got a stone wall and he'd had to leave it at condolences. Now, for a moment, he lived again in Abrams, here on the dump, the daylight going fast.

> Now, in the time of spring (azaleas, trilliums,
> Myrtle, viburnams, daffodils, blue phlox),
> Between that disgust and this, between the things
> That are on the dump (azaleas and so on)
> And those that will be (azaleas and so on),
> One feels the purifying change. One rejects
> The trash.
> That's the moment when the moon creeps up . . .

Abrams put the book down on his lap. Purifying change. . . . Was that why he'd dashed out of the house, out of his life? To reject the trash of bad faith, shaky belief, bad luck, bad times? (Two salary cuts in three years and the pension fund a mess because of the economy, because of bad management.) Between the things that are on the dump (azaleas and so on) and those that will be on the dump (azaleas and so on). . . . He knew about that dump, the one all things come to, finally, el ultimo dump. All those condolence calls, all those funeral services, one Kaddish after another. A woman of valor is a jewel beyond price . . . a man of compassion, of tzedakah, who gave to charity. . . . Oh, yes, he was well acquainted with the dump, an expert on the dump, a professional you could say.

Abrams touched his cheek where a trim, neat beard had once distinguished itself from the rest of his pale face and, of course, from most of his clean-shaven congregation. It had been more than a week since he'd been in combat with a razor. It was all stubble of varying lengths now. Non-rabbinic: anonymous.

The light had changed, become less than daylight but still more than night. Abrams looked up and saw that a batch of mattress-shaped clouds had drifted apart and the moon had unexpectedly risen. He had to laugh. The moon didn't creep up the way it does in poems, at least this moon hadn't. It had arrived, been revealed. Or was it only that Abrams was in the mood, in the market for revelations: tricky things he'd never trusted before?

The moon drifted through clouds, a movie shot. Abrams's gaze drifted up then back to the page.

> That's the moment when the moon creeps up
> To the bubbling of bassoons. That's the time
> one looks at the elephant-colorings of tires.
> Everything is shed; and the moon comes up as the moon
> (All its images are in the dump) and you see
> As a man (not like the image of a man),
> You see the moon rise in the empty sky.

Abrams particularly liked the part about the empty sky. Once the sky was truly empty could you see as a man (not like the image of a man). Portrait of the Rabbi as a Man. He'd thought that for a long time, had wondered at the completeness of his un-faith, wondered should he quit, play fair with a congregation who had the right to expect, at the least, belief from their spiritual leader.

Once, at an Oneg Shabat he'd actually tried to shock Weinstein, the president of the board, with a revelation of unbelief. Only to be greeted by a flood of postmodern bullshit, The Courage to Be, God as the Ground of Being, the kinship with the Buddha, the God within Us, Doubt as a Form of Belief. Weinstein had read Buber, he'd read Paul Tillich and Teilhard de Chardin. You couldn't turn these people off by merely telling them their rabbi didn't believe in God. This was the end of the twentieth century. If the moon was the only occupant of the night sky, that was okay with them. Nobody wanted white-bearded gods waiting in the sky anymore. Everybody was comfortable with doubt and uncertainty. Traditional observance was enough for them, and ultimate doubt only made them feel like grown-ups; all they needed was ritual—that and discourse, the endless flood of talk, opinion, interpretation. It was enough to be with other Jews. Only Abrams felt like a fake.

"Excuse me. Don't let me interrupt."

The small old man was standing there, red rheumy eyes staring at Abrams. He kept shifting his weight from one foot to another as if he, too, had to pee. But that was not his mission.

"Excuse me," he repeated. "Mary Louise and Rory and me, we wanted to ask you something."

"Yes?"

"To ask you if you would give us a sermon."

Abrams was wary. He scowled. "What's this, some kind of joke?"

A shake of the skinny head. "No, we wouldn't make a joke about that. Please."

Abrams tried not to laugh. "You're asking for a sermon? Most people just get stuck with them."

"Well, it's kind of weird being on the go. It's Sunday. And

you being a clergyman, we talked about it and wanted to ask you if you would."

Abrams was not about to get into the difference between the Christian and the Jewish Sabbath. Amused, and in some odd way saddened, Abrams knew at once he would give them their sermon, and knew what he would use as his text.

They gave him the central seat, an upturned milk can, and sat in front of him. For themselves they pulled some mattresses, stained in various, unthinkable ways, but long since dried out. Mary Louise was central, her long, ragged skirt spread around her like a gypsy queen. On her left Rory hulked. Ed, his endless fluttering stilled for once, waited on her right.

"I thought you were kidding," he began.

"Me, from a Baptist family," Mary Louise said. "Rory here, from a couple of Episcopalian atheists, and Ed's adopted but his mother was Lutheran."

"She keeps track of everything," Rory said. "Be lost without her."

Mary Louise, our lady of Rory's perpetual adoration, ignored him. She said, "Couldn't believe our good luck having a minister appear like this."

"Not a minister."

"A man of God . . . "

Abrams let it rest there. "Well," he began. "Since everybody's so different I'm not going to do a usual rabbi's sermon. I'll use a poem."

"Great," Ed said, as if every Lutheran child had expected a poem for a sermon on Sunday.

He began with the title, "The Man on the Dump," and they seemed to take its utter on-the-nose appropriateness as if he'd tailor-made it for their mutual situation. Yes, the dump, the man, here we are. They paid a perfect attention, followed him through the moon's rising, the itemization of objects on the dump, even through the slightly surreal section of dresses, stones, chains made of the worn-out dew. Then—

> One sits and beats on an old tin can, lard pail.
> One beats and beats for that which one believes.
> That's what one wants to get near. Could it after all
> Be merely oneself . . .

They seemed to like that part and Abrams paused for a little commentary, raised the question of one's beliefs being a road to who one is. Ed nodded, Mary Louise murmured something inaudible. Abrams liked the feel of still controlling a congregation, even a ragtag one of three, like this. He could always tell when a sermon was going well. This one was on track.

> . . . as superior as the ear
> To a crow's voice?

Abrams had written a poem about a crow and then had read Ted Hughes's long poem "Crow" and had torn his own piece up. The right thing to do? Wrong? Just young? It didn't matter. Apparently, once you tore something up it was in pieces forever even if you pasted it back together again.

> . . . did the nightingale torture the ear,
> Pack the heart and scratch the mind?

Abrams wondered, did it bother Stevens that Keats had already done the nightingale? Probably not. Beth used to say, with some contempt, that all poets do is talk to each other. She was probably right, they even talk to the dead ones—and they talk back. And what of his crazy idea of writing stories based on poems, what had made him stop? Fear of ridicule, of feeling foolish. Careful, don't lose your audience, speak to them, about themselves.

> . . . is it peace,
> Is it a philosopher's honeymoon, one finds
> On the dump?

He sees, from the corner of his eye, Rory smile hugely at the notion of finding peace on the dump. Abrams picks up volume and tempo, asking them to join in, to repeat some key words, phrases in responsive reading. They nod.

> . . . Is it to sit among the mattresses of the dead,
> Bottles, pots, shoes and grass and murmur aptest eve:

He pauses, inviting the responsive chant.

Mary Louise glances at her two men and they chant in unison: aptest eve. Abrams is accustomed to responsive readings in his synagogue but this is stranger. It comes out like dream-talk, like music, the sermon as abstract art. It is wild. Abrams is high; he is running a revival meeting, chamber music–style, just for three, and where better?

> Is it to hear the blatter of grackles and say
> Invisible priest; . . .

They chant in response: Invisible priest. Mary Louise's eyes are closed, her cracked lips puckered around the letter *p* in priest.

> . . . is it to eject, to pull
> The day to pieces and cry stanza my stone?

Their voices are louder now, more confident, calling out
stanza my stone as if they are three poets of the dump who want
only to have immortal longings in the shape of poems inscribed
on their tombstones when they die. Abrams takes a breath and
breathes out the last line of the poem.

Where was it one first heard of the truth? The the.

The the. What a way to phrase the truth—the the. It was like
telling all seekers to go to hell. The the. A stammer, a passionate
bad joke. God!

But the moment is too impossible, too good, to last. When
he has read the last line their interest starts to fade, he can feel
himself losing them, their attention drifting off. They think he
is stuttering. He tries a commentary on "the the" as truth but it
doesn't work. Mary Louise says she lost interest when the moon
rose in the empty sky.

"I don't want an empty sky. Too damned depressing."

"It depends on what skies you're leaving behind. And what
you trade them in for." He has no idea why but he feels as if he's
fighting for his life. With whom, three strangers, an old man
and a woman doted on by a loutish lover? All of them brought
to the dump by God knows what.

And they don't like "the empty sky." Exactly what will lib-
erate him is what they are afraid of. How can he explain to them
that it is only that freshly emptied sky that can free him, get him
off the hook, off the dump, back to life?

Abrams is tossed by nausea; he has eaten so little in the past
few days it's no wonder he's in some kind of hallucinatory state,
finding sermons in iambics, busily ungodding skies.

"Listen," he says, "I'm sorry. That wasn't much of a sermon,
using a poem and all."

They gathered around him in a reassuring chorus.

"Did me a hell of a lot of good," Rory said. "I like that part about beating on a tin can for what you believe."

"And I liked the stuff about finding peace on the dump," Mary Louise said. She stood up and shook her long skirt out, brushing away a few pebbles along with something small and crawling. "I don't believe it's true but I liked believing it."

"Well, for about a minute," Ed said. He poked at the dying fire with a stick, raising a cloud of unhelpful sparks. He spat in the embers, a hiss.

Abrams gazed at Mary Louise, at the swell of her stomach. Is she pregnant? Terrifying thought, here. How he and Beth had slaved at making a child. One final casualty had been his potency. "Too much intensity," Dr. Law had said. "Why not adopt?" Why not, indeed? Pig-headed, bull-headed, pick your animal and put its head where it didn't belong, that was Abrams on the subject.

Most awful of all were the moments when he'd tried to rouse his flagging potency by seeking out porn pictures of men making love to pregnant women. He'd not known such startling, extreme sexual things existed, but in some hidden place he understood: it was a matter of touching the woman and also the immanent child; a mixture of shame and wonder, a mad sensuality of becoming.

His three chance encounters were busy rolling up some sort of blanket—getting ready for the night? To move on? Abrams walked quietly back to the stunted tree that served as refuge. His headache was down to half its size. The brief parody of preaching had been somehow settling. But he was not finding peace on the dump. He was ready to get out, to move on, too. To find a homeless shelter, the Salvation Army—did they take rabbis, he wondered, would he have to sing Jesus loves me in order to get a meal, a clean bed, a night's sleep? What the hell! He'd given up the fantasy of a Rowena-return. That was over and it had nearly wrecked the two sisters, his marriage. But it was over. Maybe he'd just go home. The sleepier he got the nicer the idea seemed. He'd walk in, Beth so happy he was alive, no reproaches, only homecoming love.

His half-closed eyes scanned the reaches of the dump and beyond; across the railroad tracks to the shadowy outlines of some kind of stile fence, a house lovely in its simple lines, against the purplish sky, a hint of a garden blurry in the foreground. But to get to it his eyes had to take in all the rusted metal large and small, automobile fenders peeling, tin cans and bottles, greenish, moldy colors, this poisonous beauty making mounds for the eye to cross. He thought he saw the trotting figure of the dog who'd shared his first night on the dump, a tiny figure on the horizon.

Finally, what a gorgeous dump this world was, rotting, taking pleasure in its absolute decaying beauty; old, young, it didn't matter to the dump. If everything came there in the end, then it was a world, a real place, as real as Hillcrest, as his study at Temple Beth Shalom with its rickety piles of books, real as the women's reading group. All you needed was the patience to make everything fresh, young; to reject the trash amid the trash.

Where was it one first heard of the truth? The the. He'd come home from a movie, *The Three Musketeers,* a ten-year-old thrilled with honor and courage, and sat down and written a story he copied from the movie's opening scroll: A young man from Gascony set out to seek his fortune in Paris as a member of the Queen's Musketeers or some such. He'd showed it proudly to his sister who'd given it to one of her friends, a pretty, ironic girl who'd laughed and said, "This is from that movie we just saw. You stole this." Terrible mixture of truths and untruths. Honor, courage and theft. The the. Trying to write stories, his novel-in-the-drawer, all had been a wounded endeavor, somehow tainted with fakery, ever since—as complicated as making children.

Or the moment he'd decided to become a teacher of long-true truths, a rabbi, calling his father in the hospital to tell him, the old man happy with anything his son would do. Then losing courage, wanting only to sit alone in a room and make up tales to break people's hearts and make them laugh, with no heart left to call his father again, gone to join his mother by then anyway via the Laocoön tangle of tubes they give you instead of death, instead of honor and courage these days.

Or the moment the moon rose, tonight, in the empty sky. That was a kind of truth. He wished he had a pencil and paper, saw himself writing a story based on a poem as he'd wanted to do for months, maybe years; saw himself doing this in the Salvation Army shelter, or in his comfortable, book-haunted study at home—they seemed oddly interchangeable. Whichever one, it could become one of the places, times, one first heard of the truth, the the. He wanted a lot at the moment: a scotch, a beer, a steak, a soft bed. Still, to trade all of it, God included, for a pencil and paper seemed at this exhausted moment a reasonable exchange.

Abrams was falling asleep, back against the scratchy bark of the tree, his right leg stiff, tingling. His trouser cuffs were unpleasantly wet: the mysterious, ubiquitous evening dew. As waking faded, his mother appeared, her usual time for return. His mother, blessed with a witty tongue but cursed with a stammer, would have understood all that had happened to him. Laughing, doomed to a shortness of breath and life, uneducated, unread, she saw through the smooth talkers around her, but said little. Everyone in the world busily talking away, treating those who stammered as unfortunate, sad cases. But underneath the smooth, endless rabbinical discourses, the clever talk, how many hid the stammering of a lifetime, the passionate stuttering search for the moment they first heard of the truth, the stuttering search for the the, the the, the the the the the the the the the the the the the the the the the the the the the *the*.

The Dangerous Stream of Time

Inspired by "Funes the Memorious"
by Jorge Luis Borges

. . . days more crowded than Balzac, scent of the honeysuckle,
love, and the imminence of love, and intolerable remembering,
dreams like buried treasure, generous luck,
and memory itself, where a glance can make men dizzy . . .

FROM A POEM BY JORGE LUIS BORGES

When they moved to Tucson in the summer of 1970, Lendler found it hard to believe they couldn't use their swimming pool because it was too hot out. "A land of paradox," he told Darcy. "What's next: don't drink the water because it's too wet?" He'd been in a level rage before the plane had landed, all the while they searched out their new house, after they found a school for Kate. Everything confirmed his anger; nothing could short-circuit his bitterness. Not the stark surprise of a low horizon and grand sky, a circumference of strangely beautiful jagged mountains; not concern for his child, not love for his wife. Nothing. At least not until the runaway horse and the fall turned everything upside down—pain and pleasure, east and west, even past and present.

He could see Darcy working on him, telling him it was only the strangeness of being forcibly removed from New York, swiftly introduced to the Southwest sun, a scorched summer sky. He watched her sweating in the oven of dry heat to pacify him: a nine-hour drive to Santa Fe, a whiff of a new culture.

"Santa Fe is a boutique," he told Darcy. "Can you believe

they made a whole city into a goddam boutique. So charming you could die."

"Right." She smiled. "It's selling charming and I'm buying. You ought to try it."

But misery made him relentless. "I walked past a liquor store advertising Beaujolais today. The sign in the window said, Red Beaujolais French Wine. Great With Food. What's that supposed to mean? As opposed to standing in a doorway with a bottle in a paper bag?"

"Let's give the place a chance, Lew."

"Wait, you haven't heard it all. I drove past a billboard advertising a funeral home: Crestview Funeral Home. Why the view is important I'll never know. But the billboard said: Prearranged Funerals. Prearranged! What's that—as opposed to just showing up for a funeral. A Drop-in Funeral Parlor. I just don't get this town."

Before they'd left he'd made it clear to both women, Kate, eight years old, Darcy, thirty-eight, that he hated what was being done to them. He'd chanted endlessly that the case was better handled from the home office, that Ballantine, the managing partner, was an idiot, covering his ass by shuffling people around as if they were cards in a deck and he was the dealer. When Darcy told him she was counting on "tincture of time" Lendler was not appreciative. He didn't need any of those doctor's catchphrases with which her father had peppered her childhood. Later he told her he was sorry. Kate required no apology. There were horses all over New Mexico and she was an eight-year-old girl: a marriage made in heaven.

Lendler was more concerned about what he'd been doing to Darcy. Stuffing his briefcase with papers he'd paused, surprised that in the clutch he was not trusting Darcy's take on things. She had always been his reality principle. In the midst of the hurly-burly of his late-started ambitions, he often watched with admiration as she drew her own life to a more modest scale: her gallery in Soho, a class act but only open on three-day weekends; exercising her gift for drawing in life class twice a week. Years before, she'd had the impulse to move her activity to a larger arena, but they'd fought over the move—to an important gallery in Los Angeles—and the project had been a casualty of the struggle. About this move she seemed curious, interested. For Lendler it was punishment, insult and exile.

The bad signs were subtle at first. Before two weeks had passed, they had settled into their new rented home and Lendler had lugged out two great albums of family photographs; he laid them on top of the mass of papers: research, depositions, briefs. Picture after picture gleamed at him, Kodacolored, occasionally Polaroid, emblems of the past. He'd searched them out to ease the burden of passage. But they troubled more than they calmed.

There was Darcy smiling brightly in front of the everlastingly unfinished Gaudi Cathedral in Barcelona, himself next to her, only half-smiling. Was that the summer they'd had the fights and the trouble in bed, poisoning the perfect weather of their second Spanish vacation? Or was this the earlier trip, their marriage as yet unruffled, but Generalissimo Franco spoiling everything, his Guardia Civilia with carbines at the ready on every street corner—until Darcy had wept in the bright sunlight of the Plaza del Mayor, wanting to go home? He'd never dated photographs, never written the place or the occasion on the back as a hedge for memory, not his style. He was no diarist, a rotten memorializer of his own experience. Life flew by and was replaced by more life, different life. Memory had to make do as best it could.

He whipped through the pages. A pause at St. Paul de Vence: the Galerie Maeght, Kate being held aloft, in front of a Miro sculpture, by Bob Rauschenberg wearing his trademark of those years—the long red scarf trailing the ground, Johns in the background, shy, hiding behind a Calder. Kate looked to be about three, so it must have been maybe 1965, halfway into his job with Ballantine & Gold, but there was no telling for sure. To make things worse, there were lots of years for which there were no photographs at all.

Darcy and Kate bustled in. They carried silk blouses and Kate wore jodhpurs.

"Do you know what they call it when they make the horses do special exercises for show?" Kate, all excitement, didn't want him to say it but he was feeling surly and lost and he said, "Yes, it's called dressage. My father would have called it goyim naches."

"Who told you?" But she was too up to be taken down by his small nastiness. She did a whirl to show him her riding pants. When he didn't respond she asked, "When did Grandpa Jacob die?" His mind did a computer-blurred search and came up with an approximation. "About four years ago," he said. He reached for her. "Come here, National Velvet." He held her so tightly it made him realize how strange, how tight, he felt. Darcy rescued the child from his mood. "It was six years ago," she said. "February, nineteen sixty-four. Take those off now; they have to be clean for tomorrow." Darcy watched Lendler closely; it was a new way she had of looking at him, watching for the unexpected.

At the door Kate turned. "Her name was Velvet. Nobody's named National," she told him seriously.

Darcy helped him put away the albums and he told her how he hated the disorder and vagueness of past years, photos hardly helping.

"Why the picture show, tonight?"

"I don't know," he said.

"You'd better start being happy with your present or your

future. It's a very small menu they give us. There are some interesting people here. I wandered into a gallery opening the other day and there was a young woman, half-Irish, half-Mexican, a painter. She was great fun. Smart. We exchanged phone numbers."

"You're lucky. I get my local cocounsel. He of the boots and the moustache. Not great fun."

"Anyway, we could be out of here in three months if the case settles."

"Environmental cases this big don't settle so fast. We're suing the State of Arizona. Till they get to a vote in the legislature could be three years, not months. Or more."

When Darcy bent to pick up an album, Lendler held her in the middle of the rubble of loose photos falling out of casein holders, the debris of depositions.

"It's funny you remembered the date my father died. I got it wrong. Maybe the gods are punishing me for letting my life go by in a blur."

He was ashamed to tell her he'd always been hazy about details of his life's events, even the most precious ones: no appropriate years attached, and certainly not months, days, not places and times. Trips abroad, events surrounding the birth of a child, the death of a parent.

"You've been too busy doing all the things you did. My God, Lew."

"I should have taken that offer from the guy at Channel 13. That Mosley fellow. He was so awed about my youth—my days and nights at the Cedar Bar, he practically asked for my autograph."

She sat down and asked him, "Why didn't you say yes?"

"Just what I need now. Another career."

But she knew his evasions, she persisted. "No, why?"

"I didn't remember enough about those days to do a show or a book. I was sort of on the edges of things—Max's friend. I was in on a pass. It was their life. Mine hadn't started yet."

"I'm taking you skiing this weekend. Clear out the cobwebs."

"Skiing might be a risky bet just now. The gods are clearly out to get me."

"Do yourself a favor and give the gods a rest. By the way, Kate wants a dog."

"I thought she wants a horse."

"She wants to ride a horse. She wants to own a dog."

"Is that what we need? A dog to walk?"

Darcy sneezed, rapid fire, three times and gave up on him for the moment, disgusted.

"I think I'm allergic to something around here," she said.

THE HEAT WAS OVERpowering. Lendler had to get used to the idea of dashing out to his car, turning on the air-conditioning, then dashing back in five minutes when it was cool enough to drive to the office in downtown Tucson. He was managing the recovery of hundreds of thousands of documents; boring but necessary.

Taking over the job of the gods, he punished himself using regrets. He could have quit before being shipped west like a piece of office furniture—could have taken the offer to host a TV show on the Abstract Expressionists; a show from which would have grown a book—okay, it was only public TV but for Christ's sake it wasn't public access TV—it was a bona fide offer, real money, and it was about a world he'd known. Well, at least passed through.

As a young man in the fifties Lendler had bummed around longer than most, became a lawyer later than most after a decade or so of fortunate floating. For about ten years after Harvard he'd tried to be a writer, tried to run his mediocre guitar-playing into a career of sorts. But mostly he'd hung out at a bar around the corner from his furnished apartment on University and Ninth Street. What made his floating and his hanging out so fortunate was—the bar was the Cedar Bar. Scattered among the red leatherette booths, which could have been created by a painter of the Ashcan School, were a small pantheon of the new art world.

He'd been there the night Jackson Pollock had threatened to punch out Clement Greenberg if he didn't stop talking about Cezanne. "I can talk about Cezanne," he declaimed. "But you shut up about Cezanne." He'd been there the night Franz Kline had a roaring fistfight with Willem De Kooning, the Mighty Mouse of Abstract Expressionism tackling the Drunken Dutchman—sawdust and curses mixed with shouted fragments of theoretical statements about the nature of art. He'd forgotten what the fight was about; everybody was edgy, everybody full of piss and vinegar about art—what it was and what it wasn't, what it should be.

The first time Lendler had wandered in, he found his vanished high school friend Max Friedman having a drink at the bar amidst a scattered brawl of painters. Max, it turned out, was the recording angel of the Cedar Bar, the budding scholar, writing about the new pack of artists, their ideas, their manifestos, and he'd welcomed Lendler in. If Max was the artists' scribe, Lendler became their mascot, playing the guitar at Friday night gatherings at the Artists' Club, listening to their gossip—who was really at a dead end in his work, who was sleeping with the same girl as another artist but didn't know. It was a fine time and a fine place to be young—everybody was young, no matter what their age, everything was new.

The offer from Mosley at Channel 13 had cost Lendler a lot.

He'd had to pick up ten years of his young life and turn it around in his hands for a close examination.

"You'll be a troubadour of the Abstract Expressionist revolution," Mosley said. *"Masterpiece Theater,* only history not fiction."

"It didn't feel exactly like a revolution, at the time," Lendler said.

"What did it feel like? That's what you can tell us."

But how it had felt was exactly what Lendler couldn't say. The confrontation was bad news, forced him to realize how little he had retained from those days. Not just blanks where dates and events should be—even with the events in clear outline, the interior was empty of feeling. Now, crossing broad, alien streets shimmering in an excess of sun, on some shopping errand for Darcy, he wondered why it suddenly mattered so much, what he could keep from the past and what he'd lost.

On his way to a meeting, he parked the car in one of the cavernous indoor chasms that honeycombed the city and exchanged the chill of the car for the dead, still heat of the parking garage. Dashing for the nearest exit, he leaned against the elevator door. Catching his breath in the icy air-conditioning, he understood why he'd been gazing at photos with such intensity.

Feeling uprooted and badly replanted, sticking his nose in and out of the law library, he didn't trust this new succession of sunny day after sunny day. He felt robbed of a whole library of days and weathers, what passed for a life. It wasn't just that the experience of the years had gone by unnumbered, it was that the way they'd felt was gone, faded at the edges, colors no longer true, emotions distant, the tone uncertain.

Over a drink with Gary Moss, the local counsel, all moustachio, cowboy boots and bourbon, Lendler took a chance, made himself a touch vulnerable. "Do you recall," he asked, "how you felt at the big moments of your life? I mean are they still with you in any way?"

"Never look back," Gary said. "Something may be gainin' on you." The asshole probably assumed Easterners had never heard of the baseball folk wisdom of Satchel Paige, and Lendler dropped that line of talk with colleagues.

Picking up some antihistamines for Darcy, he waited for a woman in front of him to buy a pack of filter-tips and he said out loud, "Of course, smoke, my God!" In summoning up his Cedar days he'd left out the smoke. Everybody smoked then. Max squinting over the cigarette pasted loosely on his lower lip, an overweight, Jewish pastiche of a French actor, Pollock never without a butt. You breathed smoke, in those innocent, deadly days, the way you breathed air. Smoke was air, flavored air; if you smoked yourself, you enjoyed it, it soothed; if you didn't smoke, you didn't notice it. The air of rooms in the past was smoky, blue, careless; not the clean, white, concerned air of the present.

At lunchtime, a quick trip to buy a new camera.

"Please, Daddy, please. A picture of me riding horseback. I'll send one to Sandy, I'll send one to Allison."

New images might have more magic than the old ones. He would photograph Kate on her first New Mexico horse. But first came the crisis of Darcy's allergy. She laughed between sneezes, mumbled apologies while she wiped a nose running like a faucet. The antihistamines did nothing, prompting a visit to a Dr. De Miguel, overweight, the ubiquitous boots and giant belt buckle; Mexican or Chicano, Lendler couldn't tell. De Miguel sprayed Darcy's nose and stuck cotton swabs into her nostrils.

"That's cocaine in there, Missy," he said. "So don't go getting to like it too much."

Their second car, the Plymouth, was in the shop, so Lendler

had driven her and waited, browsing the bookshelves. Next to the usual medical texts there were the signs of a secret self. García Márquez, Jorge Luis Borges, Vargas Llosa, some of the younger Magical Realists. Not the usual doctor's stuff.

De Miguel noticed his interest. The treatment finished, he washed his hands and said, over his shoulder, "I'm on the board of the university. We've got the biggest collection of South American literature just about anywhere. Have you read Isabel Allende?"

Lendler had not. "I don't really understand that leap into fantasy they keep making south of the border. My fault, not theirs," he said. "Don't mind me. I'm the wrong guy in the wrong place—completely connected to things European. A hopeless case."

"You're in the Southwest, now. We'll cure you. You'll have to come to the house. I've got the real collection there."

It turned out Dr. De Miguel knew Gary Moss's wife, knew all about Lendler's arrival in Tucson, all about his background as a lawyer and before, was a collector of Twombley and even owned a small Motherwell.

He laughed at the surprise. "This is a small town for gossip," De Miguel said. "But a cosmopolitan appetite for art. And anybody who worked with those guys—"

"Not such a big deal. We were all broke in those days. One day I lent Cy Twombley—either Twombley or Rauschenberg—twenty-five bucks and I lived off the gesture for years. Three or four of them are still clients. Now, how about my poor suffering wife?"

"Yes," Darcy said, happily. "How about her?" She'd been quietly listening, delighted to see Lendler talking with interest to somebody new.

De Miguel was writing out a prescription. "She'll be all right. It's the cottonwoods. Every summer they drop their lethal white fluffy bombs onto our innocent eyes and noses. Take these, twice a day. But mostly I prescribe tincture of time. Welcome to the state of Arizona."

"Thanks," Lendler said. "That's who we're suing for three hundred million dollars."

"No sweat," De Miguel said. "You'll come to dinner."

"TINCTURE OF TIME," LENDLER mutters the next morning en route to the Kit Carson Dude Ranch, an ecstatic Kate looking like an old English riding print, breathless in the back seat.

"Calm down. He's not my father," Darcy says. "Doctors train doctors. Those phrases are immortal. Just look at this astonishing day."

It is something: sun-painted sky and black and brown low-looming mountains on either side as they drive. Hills studded with cactus plant, pitchforklike, with three or four plump, green prickly tines. The events of the next hour or so go by as in a heat-sun-dream: smells of wet straw and sweating horses, the pungent odor of manure—Kate carefully guiding her mottled pony. "This is called posting, Dad . . . " Lendler knocking off a quick succession of photographs. The leathery old guy poking him in the arm . . . "You want to try it, Mister?" and Lendler saying, out of some weird sense of being challenged, "Yeah, why not?"

His thoughts chase a crazy path. Do something new . . . change your luck . . .

Lendler turns the camera over to an alarmed Darcy. Minutes later he is on the ground. He has no memory of having fallen, no pain, only a strange sense of floating and a great sleepiness.

• • •

IN THE HOSPITAL ALL he could remember was the idea of changing his luck.

Q: Do you know where you are?
A: I'm not sure.
Q: Do you know what happened to you today?
A: No.

Actually he knew he was in a hospital—so much white-ness—white walls, white uniforms. . . . But Lendler suspected they wanted more than that from him.

A: Aren't you going to tell me what happened?
Q: You were riding a horse and you had a bad fall. Con-cussion. You don't remember that?
A: No.

Of course he recognized Darcy and Kate when they came in. How could he not? They were Darcy and Kate! They were his!

When Darcy leaned over the bed to kiss him, the kiss brought with it much more than the comforting touch of her mouth. He remembered the time she had a freak illness, high fever, in and out of comas, and he remembered leaning over in a room at Lenox Hill Hospital on Seventy-seventh Street, at exactly eight thirty-two in the morning, kissing her on the cheek, just as she was kissing him now—except he recalled it, flooded with all the emotion, the anxious concern, would she recognize him, was she in pain, was he going to lose her, recalling, no reexperiencing, the gut-grinding terror, at the same time noting the IV plugged into her arm, dangling like silent wind chimes, the slash of morning sunlight slicing across her bed, the gibberish sounding from the loudspeaker in the hospital hall. And behind or actually in the same space as these memories—this memory, because it was one experience—was the complete, undivided block of memory which included his anxious sense before meeting Darcy that he would never get married, that he would remain a solitary circler of friends and their families.

All this happened so swiftly that it seemed to have happened outside of time. It had the time-sense of certain dreams Lendler could recall, dreams in which time was infinitely swift yet infinitely elastic. It had, too, the flooding of emotion which some dreams carry—the delicious happiness or sharp panic which he would awaken to, and only as he realized it was a dream did those emotions gradually recede.

Lendler lay there paralyzed by joy. What an experience! Were there any more like that?

Q: Tell me your name.
A: Lew Lendler. Lewis.

Lendler experiments. He tunes out the white glare and buzz of the hospital and goes back to a photograph—one that had given him a hard time only a few nights ago: he and Darcy in front of the Gaudi Cathedral. It had been the first trip, without doubt, the happiest one. Darcy's smile was as mysterious as all women's smiles but born of happiness, she was happy on that Spanish day, May 10th, 1967, he knew the date and the time, one P.M., they had asked a tourist, a woman, the instant before, to take their photograph. He remembered the particular color of the woman's purse, a surprising lavender.

Q: Do you know what city you're in, Mr. Lendler?
A: City?
Q: You're in Tucson, Mr. Lendler.
A: Ah, Tucson. Right.

One last secret experiment. He ruffled through memories, browsing, until he found one to zoom in on. The day he'd decided to go to law school, the day he looked at himself in the mirror while washing his hands after taking a leak at the Cedar Bar and saw himself in thirty years, still floating, a grizzled hanger-on, sipping his white wine at gallery openings, circling the periphery, a Flying Dutchman among the artists. Lendler remembered the vinegary smell of the urinal, the caustic odor and feel of the soap from the dispenser, he remembered the date, December 14th, 1959. But most of all he had the exact feeling of the moment: a deep wave of relief at having decided to join the world, a world, a school, anything but another year of unconnected days.

> Q: You've lost your recent memory. Because of the concussion. It will probably come back. We're taking you down for more X-rays.
> A: I see.

Bullshit! Lendler thought. I haven't lost anything. I've gotten my life back. But of course he knew he must not tell them about his discovery. He wasn't sure why, he just knew he must keep it a secret.

> Q. Do you know who I am?
> A: Darcy, you're my Darcy.
> Q: And this little girl?
> A: Kate, Kate-o, when I come back from this test we'll all go home.

AND THEY DID, BUT not until two days later, all bones and blood vessels checked out, a clean bill of health except for some sore muscles and an absence of recent memory. Convalescing at home was strange. Basic information seemed to be intact: his family and who he was. But of course, those were old facts.

The first day, Darcy sat with him for five hours, Lendler

taking notes as if at a deposition. At the end of the session she'd brought him up to date and he had it down on paper.

"I'll be honest," he told her. "I seem to stop about ten years ago."

"After law school?"

"Just. But it's not simple, because I know Kate—and she came only eight years ago." About his new, mysterious gift he said nothing.

"It's okay," Darcy said. "Apparently it comes back. Piece by piece."

She'd brought him up to speed about Ballantine and the move. Not wishing to alarm anybody at the office who might alert the powers in New York, he kept up a show: papers to-ing and fro-ing by messenger, the phone ringing, the fax beeping.

In the middle of this activity, which Lendler used mainly to familiarize himself with a case that was entirely new to him, Darcy would command: "For the next hour you rest." Three times a day, in the cool, darkened bedroom with only the air-conditioner's hum for company, he reached back into his new store of treasures. Accidentally he stumbled on a special, illicit pleasure. He was treating the whole adventure as illicit, his dirty little secret. But one special nuance was particularly delicious.

He discovered that the richness of recovered experience extended, if carefully done, to the sexual. He called up Maria, the Italian girl in NYU summer school, making love behind a bush in Washington Square Park, guitar music and a half-moon for accompaniment. The smell of olives—they'd been for a drink and some nibbles at the Hotel Earle; the olives lingered on their breath. Lendler reexperienced that evening in May with perfect fidelity. Out of some mixture of anxiety and tact, he stopped the memory short of replicating an eight-year-old orgasm. That was a little too scary.

It struck Lendler that this kind of imaginative adultery was ironically perfect for a man who'd always been faithful to his wife. That was when he was still enjoying his secret, taking pleasure in getting back all the earlier, lost lives he'd been mourning; before the fear set in, before the sense of taking part in some ritual in which no one else in the world could join him; before he began to feel so alone.

In the middle of the fourth night Lendler woke, staring into the night. He had been dreaming—something about hospitals, but long ago, not here in Tucson. At this moment he was hopelessly in the dark present, as much here and now as the digital clock which gleamed 3:03 then 3:04, lonely and shivery with nothing but more seconds to look forward to. That was when he knew he needed to tell someone about what had happened to him.

"MARGARITA?"

"No, a martini, if you can do it."

"East versus West. I can certainly make a martini. Gin or vodka?"

Dr. De Miguel's bulk was shadowlike, the sun at his back. He mixed and poured while Lendler told his tale.

"Your wife—Daisy . . . "

"Darcy."

"She doesn't know about this. About this new gift."

"I'm not so sure it's a gift. No, she doesn't even know I'm here. She thinks I'm at the law library."

A cocker spaniel loped into the room. He was large, his brown floppy ears flapping, and he filled the room with a rank outdoors doggy smell. De Miguel grabbed him and wrestled affectionately for a moment. Two more animals tumbled in: a black and white terrier and a black Labrador.

"You like dogs," Lendler said. "In a big way."

"This is nothing. I used to have dozens. Almost did me in, that passion."

Lendler accepted his martini. "How can a passion for dogs do you in?"

"I was teaching at Arizona State, over in Tempe, outside of Phoenix. I never wanted to practice, just teach: anything, biology, ethology, medicine. Surrounded by dogs and students, I became fascinated by the minds of animals, of my dogs. I was convinced that it was wrong to say that dogs don't have thoughts and beliefs about their world just because they might be different from our beliefs."

"Beliefs?"

"Not just beliefs. An emotional and intellectual life. This fellow here—when he makes a mess on the carpet he feels guilty, the way I would have if my mother'd caught me doing it. I had a hunting dog once who used to play jokes on me. I'd throw a stick for him to fetch and he'd pretend not to know where it was in the tall grass. Then when I got near him he'd dash right to it and look at me with a grin."

"Do dogs grin?"

"This one did. And humor, playing jokes, is one of the basic human traits in my book. I began running experiments, trying to publish what people thought were outrageous results. I had the idea, I still have it, that every living being, dogs, lizards, monkeys, people, they all live in time, which means they live in a story, a narrative frame. They make sense of their lives in terms of past, present, a future. Now, obviously some narratives are more complicated than others. But all animal life—ours included—is based on narrative." De Miguel emptied his glass. "They threw me out, finally. Must have figured I was on to some Mexican mystic crap. So I picked the simplest specialty I could find, and moved to Tucson." He laughed. "Even after I got here, my obsession cost me. Somebody I loved thought I was crazy. She threw me out, too."

"How awful."

A heavy shrug. "People with obsessions are hard companions."

Lendler was delighted by the distraction of someone else's obsession. If he could have held off talking about his own situation forever, he would have happily done it, with talk of dogs and beliefs; narrative; of the cost of fixed ideas.

De Miguel pushed one of the dogs aside and moved to the bookcase along the wall.

"Rude of me to run on like this, when you came here because you're so troubled. I'm not sure how much I can help—but maybe I can throw a little light on what's happened to you. Not necessarily scientific light—just light."

"It's kind of you to see me, Dr. De Miguel. Right now any illumination will be gratefully accepted."

"Call me Alvaro. You didn't come to me because I'm a doctor. You have doctors, neurologists, the others." He ran his hand over the spines of books, searching.

"It's hard to say why I came. I'm scared about losing memory and scared about getting so much back from so long ago. I haven't met many people here and I needed to talk. You didn't seem the usual medical man. Those South American books in your office—all those Magical Realists."

"I can understand why you'd be frightened. Your memory has turned the natural order of things inside out. It's usually one of the terrors of growing old."

De Miguel extracted a book carefully and held it up to the light. "I have another pet theory," he said. "I think that everything in life happens twice. The first time, in books, the second time, in life."

A surprise for Lendler. "Not the other way around? I thought writers write from their experience."

De Miguel sat down next to him on the couch. "The good ones write from their imagination, more." A great bulk of a sigh. "I wanted to be a writer more than anything else. I wanted to combine Darwin and Chekhov. Did you know that Rimsky-Korsakov was a doctor, too? Anyway, instead, now I just keep people breathing and swallowing."

"Pretty important stuff."

He handed Lendler the book. "So is this stuff," he said.

Lendler took the book. It was opened to a story called "Funes, The Memorious." The first line read: "I remember him (I scarcely have the right to use this ghostly verb; only one man on earth deserved the right and he is dead) . . ."

THAT NIGHT, KATE AND Darcy asleep, he begins the strange nine-page story written by a blind Argentinian. The man called Funes is an Argentinian farm boy, his father a horse-breaker. In the course of one night the narrator spends with Funes, the boy tells of being thrown from a horse in the rain.

"Previous to the rainy afternoon when the blue-tinted horse threw him, he had been—like anyone—blind, deaf, mute, somnambulistic, memoryless . . . For nineteen years, he said he had lived like a person in a dream: he looked without seeing, heard without hearing, forgot everything—almost everything. On falling from the horse he lost consciousness; when he recovered it, the present was almost intolerable it was so rich and bright; the same was true of the most ancient and trivial memories . . ."

Lendler rests the book on his chest, the story unfinished. It was not quite his story, but similar enough to feel eerie. Lendler's present was not "rich and bright," it was simply cut off from the rest of his life, especially from recent time. The excitement over filling in all the dim places of the past with memory, with feeling, had yielded to the awful sense of strangeness. It came with a price—the years of happiness with Darcy, of Kate, of delayed and enjoyed success, of money in the pocket, of money starting to pile up in reserve, a first for Lendler—all the happiness of the past ten years was in danger of being erased, like a mistake on a tape.

". . . He remembered the shapes of the clouds in the south at dawn on the 30th of April of 1882, and he could compare them in his recollection with the marble grain in the design of a leather-bound book which he had seen only once . . . These recollections were not simple; each visual image was linked to muscular sensations, thermal sensations . . . Two or three times he had reconstructed an entire day . . . *I have more memories in myself alone than all men have had since the world was a world . . .*"

Would that include the memories of Alvaro De Miguel's dogs, Lendler wondered. And did each of those animals have strong and weak memories; troubling ones and happy ones as each of their narratives unfolded, day by day, year by year? No one in New York would ever think about animals this way. You had to come west for that.

Reconstruct an entire day, Lendler thinks. Only a god could do that. But the fear and loneliness which had grabbed him in the middle of the night was suddenly gone. Funes and his fall from a horse a hundred or so years ago gave him comfort. Dr. De Miguel apparently knew his remedies. Lendler was no Funes, no cosmic prodigy of memory—but somewhere some crossed wires in his brain had been connected, with mysterious results. His thoughts drift to Mosley, the slim, intense, chain-smoking young man from public television whose offer had thrown Lendler into such panic.

Smoke! He is actually smelling the smoke from Mosley's cigarette. No one in the house smokes; it has to be the smoke of memory, the same smoke that filled the Cedar Bar all those young years.

THE NEXT DAY LENDLER calls Mosley from his office to ask about the TV project, the book, is it all still of interest.

"Still up for grabs," Mosley says. "Change your mind?"

"Could be. But I'm living in Tucson for the moment. I'll be here till this case settles."

With the cheerful optimism of television Mosley speaks smoothly of phones and faxes and jets and Federal Express.

"Where you are doesn't matter. It's what you remember and how you can get it down. Don't forget, we'll have a writer assigned to the project, as soon as you give us enough material to start archival research. All we need is for you to give us the shape of that whole wild period. My God," Mosley was on a delighted roll, "look at the present scene, the art scene. What a vacuum. Have you strolled around Soho or Fifty-seventh Street lately? Nobody knows what anybody else is doing—only what they're selling. No ruling spirit, no idea. The new is empty. You'll tell us what it was like when it was full."

"Right," Lendler answers with a brisk confidence. It is a confidence borrowed from Dr. Alvaro De Miguel and his Indian friend Señor Ireneo Funes the memorious.

"Let's talk about money," Mosley says, exhaling smoke into the phone. Later he will think about Mosley and his complaints about the empty present. What did the man expect? The present is always empty. It takes time to fill it.

THE PROJECT IS A fine distraction from Lendler's mind-watching. Bits and pieces of recent memory have been creeping back. He recalls joining Ballantine & Gold, he remembers coming to

Tucson, rages and all. Watching his mind is like shining a flash-light inside a dark cave and slowly rotating it. It is not a lot of fun.

But the beginning of the Mosley project is thrilling: digging out old papers, talking into a tape recorder Darcy has happily bought for him; she is delighted with the project, perhaps for hidden reasons of her own. He doesn't care. Finally he has no interest in anyone else's mind but his own. The kinds of losses and gains his fall has put him through have concentrated his attention. For the moment, the interior landscape of his mind has become the universe. He has reduced life and time to one dimension: the past.

He remembers how to play chess with the clarity of the eighteen-year-old who'd learned it in Washington Square Park, playing against sophisticated homeless people, respecting their skill but careful to sit downwind from those who'd not had the blessing of hot water and soap for weeks. He starts to play chess with Darcy. A fresh way for them to connect in this alien environ-ment. He goes back to his labors of memory with fresh energy.

BUT, AS IT DEVELOPED, the process was not entirely under control.

"Max wants to see you," Sis Friedman had said on the phone. "It has to be soon." Lendler recalls the exact tone: urgent but not wanting to frighten him. He knew Max had a heart condition, his old enemy in whose face he kept smoking and drinking. Tough Max, young and old, his own man, always.

"Where is he?"

"New York Hospital."

The excitement of making sense of the inpouring of days and nights was interrupted by the memory of Max's last days, of how Lendler had not found the courage to face up to Max's death—something being done so elegantly by Max, himself.

He'd never gone to the hospital. At the funeral he lurked at the back of the chapel hoping nobody would notice him, a criminal at the scene of the crime. It was a kind of dark coda to the music of the excitement of Eighth Street, of the Stable Gallery, of Friday nights at the Artists' Club, of all-night drinking parties under the trees in the Springs, of Pollock's awful death in that car wreck—all of it. Would Mosley want to put Max's death into his film?

He could have expected some feeling of regret, of nostalgia. What was astonishing was the awful grief. All he'd had to do was go to the hospital to see his old friend—he hadn't even called him. It choked him, like swallowing a drink the wrong way. Kate found him sitting at the desk weeping.

"What is it, Dad? What's the matter?"

"I'm sorry kiddo. I just remembered something from a long time ago?"

"Something bad?"

"Yes, bad."

Kate called Darcy, who'd never seen Lendler in tears. She phoned the neurologist, who told her to bring her husband to the emergency room, where he would meet them. When they arrived, the neurologist was waiting. Short, ruddy complexion, brazenly cheerful.

Q: Mr. Lendler, what is upsetting you?

A: I've been thinking about certain things which happened.

Q: Happened, when?

A: Years ago.

Q: What are these "things"?

A: Regrets. Don't you have any regrets?

Q: Are you angry? Why are these regrets so upsetting now?

A: I don't know.

Q: Ah.

The neurologist turns to Darcy.

Q: After a concussion we see all sorts of reactions. I'll give him something to make him feel better for now. And then, we'll need some more tests.

A: I want to see Dr. De Miguel.

Q: Who is Dr. De Miguel?

A: Dr. Alvaro De Miguel.

Q: You mean the ear-nose-throat man? But he's not a neurologist.

A: That's the one.

Q: He's the one with those crackpot theories about dogs and such.

A: Absolutely!

IT WAS DARCY'S FIRST dinner party in Tucson. To give it a semblance of normalcy, make it less like a consultation, she invited Lila Moreno, the young painter she'd met at a gallery, downtown.

"It's a little unfair to her," she'd told Lendler. "She'll be the only one who doesn't know what's been going on or why we're having the dinner with Dr. De Miguel."

"There's Kate."

"Kate's eating early and going to see *The Little Mermaid* for the twentieth time with a sitter."

Lendler had told her everything on the way back from the emergency room; almost everything. He'd left out the reexperience with Maria in Washington Square Park. But he gave her the story about Funes to read. He wasn't sure she understood it all. But, Darcy-like, she'd set about trying to help. The dinner party with Dr. De Miguel was her way. Neither of them was exactly sure of what they wanted from the evening but Lendler wanted to talk to Dr. De Miguel and felt too foolish to consult him again, as if he were an unpaid psychiatrist. Darcy bought a Tex-Mex cookbook and set about her task.

THE SURPRISING DR. DE Miguel had brought his black Labrador, Ric-Rac, to Kate's joy. The second surprise of the evening was Lila Moreno. De Miguel had arrived first and he and Lendler were standing around in the kitchen while Kate teased Ric-Rac, when Darcy brought in the woman with astounding platinum hair. Without hesitation she walked up to De Miguel and kissed him on the mouth. Then, enjoying the fuss, she announced, "Alvaro and I lived together for three wonderful years."

De Miguel coughed into his margarita. "I didn't know you thought they were wonderful."

The evening moved into high gear after that and stayed there. The problem of Lendler's extraordinary memory, its pleasures and terrors, was brought out and put on the table, part of the fare for the evening along with the prosciutto and melon flavored with peppercorns.

"It probably feels as if a too-perfect memory is a forbidden thing. A taboo is being violated," De Miguel said. "It could be what's frightening you."

Darcy poured dangerously powerful margaritas from a pitcher and said, "If it's forbidden, maybe that's why Funes dies at nineteen."

"And already looks like an ancient monument," Lila said.

"You know the story too?" Lendler asked.

"It's one of Alvaro's favorites. He loves the mysteries of memory."

"I've never forgotten you," De Miguel said, intimate, as if the two of them were alone.

"You have your dogs and your noses." She laughed and blew a kiss across the table. Nobody was embarrassed. The margaritas were insurance against that. The women sipped theirs. The two men, the doctor and the patient, gulped, poured, and drank again as if they were taking in water in the desert.

"Nobody seems to know much about these neurological things in the brain," Lendler complained.

"Wrong," De Miguel said. "They've isolated the seat or seats of memory, they know which areas secrete which kinds of memories. They know an amazing amount. The problem is—they can't do much about it. They'll tell you, 'The functions you've lost may come back gradually.'"

"They've told me," Lendler said to his glass, gloomy, working on getting high but only getting lower.

By the time the apple pie peppered with jalapeños was served, De Miguel was loftily high enough for all of them. He rose and circled the table, glass in hand, one of the healing gods gone wild.

"We have been asked here to try to help our new Eastern friend Lew Lendler in the grip of his mysterious experience. I hope you don't think I gave you the story of Funes, that monster of memory, because I thought his was a wonderful fate. I only wanted to ease the terror—once something has been conceived of, has been written down, it may be less frightening."

Lendler raised his eyes over his own glass. "What do you think about what happened to Funes, to me?"

"I think it's rotten. Listen to this." He produced the Borges book from somewhere, from nowhere, and read: 'In effect Funes not only remembered every leaf on every tree of every wood, but even every one of the times he had perceived or imagined it. He determined to reduce all of his past experience to some seventy thousand recollections, which he would later define numerically. Two considerations dissuaded him: the thought that the task was interminable and the thought that it was useless.' All men, all women, are artists of experience," De Miguel said, still circling. He was behind Lila's chair now. "Each of us have our lives to arrange and rearrange in our minds, in memory. Even my darling dogs probably recall everything but without fine distinctions. But to recall everything with equal clarity is to make a child's story out of a rich and strange novel. The dimming of the past is as natural as the sun waning each day. To lose that dimming and the comparative brightness of the recent past is like having a day without a night to follow."

"Alvaro doesn't just make speeches, he sings arias," Lila said. "He's one of the great ranters. Like Don Quixote. He can convince anybody of anything."

"Now that you know the problem, now that you have the problem in your flesh, you have to find a way to refuse the memory that pains you—and nurture the memory you want, that you need. You have to step out of the loop you're in, somehow, anyhow."

The words came from a margarita-heightened loftiness, descending with authority on Lendler waiting below.

"He even commanded me to become a painter—so I did," Lila said.

"And left me in the bargain," De Miguel mourned.

"Not that old song, Alvaro. One more word and I'll come back."

He added one more word. "Come."

Lendler rose. He, too, had a tequila song to sing. He told of surprise griefs waiting behind unexpected delights in the jungle of the past; of regrets and reproaches for mistakes, failures, for being the wrong kind of man at the wrong moment in time, over and over again—the kind of man without the courage to help a friend as he died. He told them how awful it was to be able to recover those moments, with perfect artistry, without being able to change them even a little. Better the pleasures of ordinary, daily amnesia.

"Once I saw an old movie on television. It was about Lister, the man who invented ether as an anesthetic. The actor who played Lister was about to amputate a man's leg, before the invention, to show how horrible it was, how much the world needed a general pain-killer for surgery. He leaned over the poor patient and said something I never forgot. 'All I can offer you,' he said from behind his surgical mask, 'is the fact that pain has no memory.' "

Lendler is determined not to weep again. "But my discovery is what everybody knows sooner or later—that memory has pain." By an effort of will he grins at them, small tears reflecting in the corners of both eyes, as Kate runs into the kitchen, home from the movies, eager to play with Ric-Rac. De Miguel, moved by Lendler's song, is drunk enough to embrace him. Darcy puts her arms around both of them; the trio sways. Into this Lao-coön's tangle Lila Moreno inserts herself.

"Come, Alvaro," she says. "I'd better drive you home."

"Will you stay with me?"

"Yes," she says. "You think I enjoy living away from you? But I'll only stay for a few years." She explains to Lendler and Darcy, "I can only handle his craziness a few years at a time."

Before he allows her to lead him to her car, De Miguel gives the black Labrador to an ecstatic Kate. Over Darcy's protests he says, "She wants a dog and I have too many. Ric-Rac won't forget me. That's all I ask." Overwrought by the evening's intensity, by the unaccustomed tequila, Darcy sits among the dirty dishes and cries. It is Lendler's turn to comfort her.

• • •

IN THE MORNING THERE was the monumental headache at the base of Lendler's skull. But there was also a new determination. He had his orders from De Miguel: step out of the loop. He would not be at the mercy; he would take charge. How to do this was, however, not exactly clear.

He called Ballantine in New York and ran a quick review of the progress of the case, reciting by rote, quoting from friendly and unfriendly depositions, not completely understanding what he was saying. He relied on old skills and language. He brought it off, though Ballantine, understandably, was not quite sure why he'd called.

Then, out into the streets of Tucson. No lingering around in stillness, a sitting duck for uncontrolled memory, his consciousness tiptoeing in a mine field. Yesterday's secret pleasures were this morning's terrors. Keep moving. He carried a camera slung around his neck, a time-traveling tourist in the present, snapping off quick shots to prove to himself that he'd been where he was.

For a while he just observes the line of cars moving along the broad avenue which would become Interstate 10—they move forward, like moments and hours traveling forward, steady, inevitable.

In the glare of the noon sun, ignoring the heat which frames buildings in that Western sun-shimmer of hallucination, Lendler leans against a metal fence festooned with bright red and yellow posters promising Native American art exhibitions. He removes the camera from around his neck. It is a fifteen-year-old Rolleiflex, too large by recent standards, but a class act; veteran of important and trivial moments, Italian vacations, a wedding or two, old, memorializing friend. Carefully, Lendler swings it on the leather sling and smashes it against the fence several times.

The sound is louder than he expected. There are only two people getting into a car nearby in the killing noon heat. Neither seems to notice the extraordinary thing Lendler has done. He dumps the shards, dangling film and all, in a trash can on the corner and moves on, sweating but cool. It is a beginning, he thinks. The moment, 12:14 by his digital watch, is electric in its presence. He has begun to step out of the loop.

In the camera store, cool and quiet, Lendler examines the state of the art in photographic memory. He is not sure why he is there, holding elegant Nikons, smoothly rounded Rolleiflexes, a tiny Canon with a zoom lens. When he slips the small instrument into his pocket he holds his breath; he is going so far he may not know the way back. At the door there is a shrill, terrifying beeping that tells him how far he has actually gone.

"I need to call someone," he told the security officer who walked him carefully to the rear of the store.

"A lawyer?"

"No."

DE MIGUEL TOOK CHARGE quickly. He wasted no time asking Lendler why he'd done it. He addressed himself at once to the beefy, irritable young man in charge of security.

"I'm a doctor," he said and handed over his card. "This man is an attorney, do you know what that means?"

"Sure."

"It means he's an officer of the court. Counselor Lendler, here, has just come to Tucson to live. If you bring the police into this, he'll be finished."

"Nobody said police," the security man said. "But he stole a camera worth four hundred and fifty dollars. Some lawyer!"

"He didn't steal it. It's still here. Look at his wallet. Six charge cards including Visa and American Express. He'll buy it now."

THE CAFÉ WAS SO dark after the dazzling sunlight, Lendler could only make out De Miguel's round outline. "That was some performance you put on," he said.

"That was some trick you pulled. How about a margarita."

"It's awfully early."

"I think on an occasion like this early or late doesn't mean much." He commanded two margaritas.

After a moment Lendler said. "You won't say anything to Darcy."

"What were you trying to do? Why a camera?"

"I don't know. I smashed my old one. On purpose."

"Smashed it. Why?"

"Maybe I just wanted to stop the endless cycle of records and reflections. Tabula rasa. Just start cold. Out of the loop, like you said."

"But why not buy a new one? Why steal?"

A tough question. But Lendler poured out whatever came to mind. If he got caught he could be disbarred, if he couldn't be a lawyer anymore they would probably pick up and go back to New York and start over; he tossed in the Mosley project and then his growing panic at the miserable surprises waiting for him in the shadows of his new gift. It was all a dumb attempt at an escape.

"I know it's all craziness. Partly your fault. You told me to get out of the loop."

"As is frequently the case these days, I was drunk."

"Taking back your advice?"

"No. But I meant the mind, the soul. Not smashing and stealing things."

"I think I was trying to short-circuit what's been going on."

De Miguel was mellowing. He sipped and said, "Maybe it is that simple. Real generosity towards the future consists in giving all to the present."

"Did you make that up?"

"No," De Miguel said.

"How about generosity to the past?"

"The same thing."

"I haven't thanked you for coming down and saving my ass. Pulled you away from your patients."

A wave of De Miguel's hand. "They're covered. Doctors always cover."

Lendler felt the start of one of the panic memories. He quickly ordered another drink. De Miguel joined him. The minty taste and the salt along the rim distracted Lendler's tongue and attention for a moment. But the memory was a bad one from May 1964: four years after the marriage, the bad time, after the second trip to Spain; Darcy had gotten an offer to run an elegant gallery in Pasadena.

She asked him to go with her, to let her have this chance—and he'd said no, not wanting change at that moment. Darcy-like, after one flare-up, she'd been quietly unhappy, subtly cooler towards him and strangely harder on herself. Remembering his heedlessness, the unthinking cruelty to Darcy—was like putting his tongue on a rotting, aching tooth. It was not ordinary remembering—it flashed the pain through him, combining the immediacy of reliving the moment with the knowledge of the resulting pain to come and the awful information that you couldn't use what you knew to go back and do it differently—unbearable to think what misery he'd given her by hanging tough at a central moment for her; a misery that hadn't softened until Kate came along. "Funes, you poor son-of-a-bitch," Lendler thought, "how did you live as long as nineteen with a memory like that? How could you stand it?"

He muted the feeling with another margarita, another one after that, spiced with talk about the mysteriousness of the Southwest after a New York life, about Lendler's fall and how to rise from it, about how his recent memory had been returning, more each day, about De Miguel's past recaptured with Lila. Lendler asked De Miguel about the writer, Borges, and De Miguel said he'd been blind much of his life, a librarian in Buenos Aires, and Lendler drank again, half toast to the blind creator, half blind need of his own.

With each drink the afternoon congealed around them; with each new round it became clearer that Lendler still had something important to do to step out of the loop and back to safety.

DE MIGUEL WATCHED FROM the sidewalk as Lendler walked into the traffic. For one brief instant some of the drivers stared, amazed at what they saw, a man wearing a suit and tie carefully walking onto the highway, as cars braked or swerved, then lying down on the white line in the middle of the baking midday heat. One minivan swerved to avoid hitting him, another car braked too fast and almost clipped the rear end of the car in front.

On the corner, leaning against a lamppost, Dr. Alvaro De Miguel watched Lendler's progress. He understood; he approved. He saw the scene precisely the way Lendler had explained it to him as they left the café. The push of cars, the endless automotive stream as the flow of remembered time, moving forward on one side, backward on the opposite side. But, what would happen if an unprotected human being—Lendler— was introduced into the equation? A kind of performance art, whose gesture was, of course, not without risk.

Lendler lay exquisitely calmed by tequila and let the sun bake him, for an instant, as if he were an inanimate object, a thing in the way of other moving things. Mindless, at last, he remembered nothing; nothing hurt and nothing was required of him. Over or under his closed, sweating eyelids, yellows and reds hovered and when he opened his eyes the horizon trembled in its haze of heat.

All around him a chaos of horns and tearing sounds of sudden brakes made marvelous music. Miraculously, as in a slow-motion dream, no car struck another in the skidding ballet. Lendler rose and, carefully threading his way through the helter-skelter of steaming metal and wheels, left the scene before the imaginary threat of the far off police siren could become real.

LENDLER DRESSED QUIETLY AND was stepping swiftly out of the bedroom, carrying his new, hard-won, super-duper camera, when Darcy called out and asked him to come back to bed.

"Lew, let's go back to New York." Her voice was alert, clear. She'd probably been up watching him dress. Lendler sat on the edge of the bed. He touched her cheek; it was still warm with sleep. "I thought you like it here." He said nothing about yesterday's camera or highway adventures.

"It's you," she said. She shook her head as if to clear it. "They have different doctors in New York. I don't know." She clutched at him, confused. Without getting undressed again he touched her in ways they both remembered with pleasure and they made love with uncomplicated joy for the first time in many months.

In the middle, she said, "Are you here? Are you?"

"You can't get any here-er than this."

"Sometimes," she said.

• • •

THAT NIGHT LENDLER PROWLS through the house with the new camera. He has never before noticed the elegant moulding on the ceilings; the archway to the dining room is covered by a sprawl of sculptured grapes; there are interesting details everywhere. He photographs Kate playing with her dog in a shapely bay window in her room. The next day at lunch he drives to the tram for tourists which runs up into the Columbian Mountains.

There has been an unusual amount of rain and the usually dry, brown little arroyos in the tram's path are flooded, running like tiny waterfalls. The three-pointed cactus is everywhere surrounded by grass. A brown and white deer with a muzzle like an Indian mask runs from the covered tram before Lendler can photograph it, but he takes pictures of everything else, including a roadrunner, famous from cartoons in his childhood; he takes three rolls.

A few nights later he is placing the shots of the house and the mountains into a new album. Darcy looks over his shoulder, surprised.

"What's this?" she asks.

Lendler smiles. "A collage of calm."

"Of everything new."

"Same thing."

Later, alone, he gazes at the photographs, but his mind is buzzing with details of the day: he is up to speed on the case, the judge has ordered a prompt presentation of evidence; there is a slight hope of an early settlement. Lendler feels no urgency, no echo of old rage. He pulls out the old album and opens it, looking at each picture carefully, fearful of an explosion of pain: Lendler and Max standing with De Kooning and a young woman wearing a big hat, outside the Eighth Street Playhouse.

He does not remember who the young woman was, though she looks familiar. Max is—just Max, his old friend, long gone. All the pictures are again slightly dimmed, vague emblems of past times; stills from a movie whose plot he recalls only in outline. Comfortably he thinks, Mosley will have to find someone else to tell that story.

He feels lucky, not just to have escaped the police; lucky that the high flood of old, vivid memory is receding; lucky to have escaped the fate of poor Ireneo Funes, ancient at eighteen, dead at nineteen, murdered by a crushing weight of memory. Lendler had been sent to Tucson by Ballantine's corporate whim. But his fall from the horse was his own accident.

And he has learned what he's learned, the same way he's ever learned anything: by accident. Some blessings bring their own curse; to get rid of one you had to lose the other. He would stay in the ordinary, dangerous stream of time. There would be new obligations, new claims, before the dust of the present settled into memory—like the new, entirely real presence of Ric-Rac, a black huddle with his funky smell of damp dog-hair, sleeping near Lendler's desk.

The moments of every new day came last in sequence of time, but in truth they come first. And, for the moment, Lendler is happy—in this house, with this family, in the strange new city of Tucson where everything is new and nothing yet demands to be remembered.

Questions and Answers

Inspired by "The Second Coming,"
a poem by W. B. Yeats

T hat was the last year in New York when the answers out-numbered the questions. You remember that year!

It was the year Orbach yo-yoed between New York and Washington trying to escape his misery at breaking up with Ruth by teaching, then back to pursue Ruth, then back to Washington, finally enmeshed in that trouble with the student. This was only eight months after he'd dashed to Washington to teach at Georgetown Law. Now he was tangled up in an action against a young woman who'd brought a copy of Monarch Notes—the little blue book that would illegally help her with the answers to test questions—into a classroom quiz on Yeats's poem "The Second Coming," that savage little piece Orbach had always cherished.

The offender was a Czechoslovak young woman named Geneva Brask whose father worked at the embassy. Orbach could not believe he was tangled up in this ugly foolishness. He was not a genuine academic, only a New York lawyer with an extra Ph.D. in Literature and Law—an adjunct professor—a part-timer, no tenure track, no Major Medical. Everything was a first for him, especially this encounter.

"Why did you do that?" Orbach had asked Geneva Brask.

"I have to pass. I need the answers."

"But it wasn't that kind of test. Just an informal review."

"Answers!" she had said, actually shutting her bloodshot blue eyes to avoid Orbach's irritated gaze. "I am sorry," she repeated. "Answers!" Somehow the fact that she was very pretty and kept running her tongue over her attractively chapped lips made Orbach even more uncomfortable. He thought she looked a little like his ex-wife, Ruth, but he thought a hundred women a week looked like Ruth.

When the spring term was almost over Jeffrey Jarman took him out to dinner. Jarman was the one buddy Orbach had made in Washington. You couldn't call him a friend; everything about him was so ambiguous that friendship would have constituted a restrictive category—God forbid! Faculty Buddy was better—a looser category.

"How can you afford this kind of a dinner out on a professor's salary?"

This kind of dinner was at The Bistro in the Woods, in Virginia. You know the place. Twenty-eight dollars an entrée, vegetables a la carte, profoundly dark, big fish tank near the cash register. Jarman smiled at him over the gigantic menu. "I can't afford the apartment I keep in New York, either," he said. "The trick is not to ask those questions. Then you don't have to answer them. Especially not to yourself." After which he offered Orbach his pied-à-terre on East Seventy-fourth Street for as long as required. It was perfect timing; money was an issue, adjunct teaching paying the way it did.

Jeffrey Jarman was big on answers too, only he had them one after another instead of all at once: serial intellectual monogamy. Jarman had dazzled and then troubled Orbach by championing every possible academic style and point of view, in turn. Nothing canceled anything else out. All was possible—

even perhaps true, or true enough. Structuralism held a key to understanding language—even in the law. Deconstruction could extend Freud into new and wonderful pathways. There *was* a self or the self had vanished in the nineteenth century, depending on where Jarman was that week or year. His field was supposed to be history, but like a great jazz pianist, he could play anything if you just whistled him a few bars.

"It's what's so nice about teaching," he told Orbach. "The horizon keeps receding, so you don't have to hand out compass points telling everybody where they are. Which, of course, is what they really want, alas."

Which is when Orbach told him about the cheating incident.

"I wanted to tell her I didn't give a damn about answers. That this was about legal ethics in literature—but she didn't care about the Celtic twilight or post-Christian imagery. She had to have answers."

"Was she pretty?"

Orbach nodded, glum.

"That always makes it tougher."

"I would have dropped the whole thing," Orbach said. "But just my luck there was a hotshot guy in the class who's running for something in student government and he turned the Czech girl in and he's holding on like a dog with a bone."

Later, over the poire eau-de-vie, Jarman said, "Don't let that stuff get to you. Teaching is an acrobatic stunt—every idea, every theory, every method is just a place to balance yourself at the edge of the high wire; you rest, gather your strength, and start walking it again. You could hand out those Monarch ponies along with the test and it wouldn't make any difference."

"She was a pretty good student till then," Orbach said. "I feel lousy. Besides, there's going to be a flap because her father works in the Czechoslovak Embassy."

Jarman said, "They're used to that at Georgetown. Everybody's father works in somebody's embassy. Not to worry. Listen, you were never a dedicated Mister Chips. Are you ever going back to New York?"

"After intersession—papers, final grades . . ."

"I mean—are you going *back*?"

"I don't know. I thought maybe I'd find a lot of answers at a university. I thought everybody here would have a particular take on the world. Historical, biographical, literary, philosophical. God, I sound like Polonius."

"And you figured you could pick your take."

"Sort of. Maybe give me some ways of figuring out what went wrong with me and Ruth."

"And instead you got a pretty girl cheating on you with a trot."

Jarman stared at him with clear blue eyes of Scandinavian descent, eyes unbleared by two Beefeater martinis, a half-bottle of Beaujolais and a thimbleful of poire eau-de-vie. "You'd better go back and stay in New York," he said.

"Why?"

"Because everybody in New York has a 'take.' Everybody in New York knows the score—and can sing it without a wrong note."

"How do you know all this?"

"It's why I don't live there. In that scrimmage of opinion I always found myself thrown for a nine-yard loss. My second wife was from New York. Still is. All I held onto was the pied-à-terre— just to keep up on the latest scores." He tossed some keys on the table. "Here you go, buddy. One opens the top lock and one the bottom." Jarman laughed. "I never can keep it straight as to which."

• • •

THAT WAS THE YEAR yo-yoing had, for the moment, replaced long-term direction. A lot of his friends kept yo-yoing back and forth to New York for projects. A few friends had what you could call "careers"—Sonny Sondheim was in research, Orbach's brother, Hiram, was in municipal bonds, Alan Day was a film distributor—but so many, like Orbach, had only projects. A twist of the wrist and Orbach was back in New York.

In the New York spring April is the coolest month. Orbach had brought the wrong clothes, short-sleeved polo shirts and chinos. He was ready for a city of warmth but it wasn't ready for him; he found a sweater in Jarman's bedroom dresser to protect him against the city he wanted to warm up to once more. Jarman's apartment was small and spilling over with books. The bookcases were all neatly alphabetized, nothing out of place. There was only one mysterious touch. The section on history was labeled Fiction and before he finished laughing at this Orbach checked the fiction shelf; sure enough it was labeled History. The question of answers was being nicely finessed in the Jeffrey Jarman style.

Orbach's plan was to insert himself back into his friends' lives quickly and painlessly. But much had changed. When he called to invite Sonny Sondheim and Martha Graves out to dinner he found they were no longer speaking. Israel was the question—or rather which answer was the question.

Sonny Sondheim had the liberal answer—Sonny who had refused to be Jewish until she was thirty-five and now was an advisor to Jewish leaders, a lecturing and fund-raising companion to rabbis. Her friend Martha Graves had *always* been Jewish and she was equally and absolutely certain about the other answer: don't give the Palestinians an inch. The two women Orbach had counted on to smooth his way back into the old circle didn't speak anymore. Impasse. Actually, by "the old circle" he'd meant Ruth; they were all friends and his plan had been to enlist Sonny and Martha in an early move on Ruth. Well, he could always do it one by one, starting with Sonny Sondheim, who was, however, booked for ten days.

Orbach's brother Hiram had always been closer to Ruth than to his younger brother. At The Westbury on Madison, Orbach tried martinis and a plea for diplomatic overtures. Hiram would not be at a loss for answers. In the eighties, brokers flying to the moon with pots of gold and others finally crashing to the ground in striped suits, strangling with legal fees, Hiram had the answer. The answer to the criminality plague eating away at the business and political world: just give and take enough rope, and decency would finally win out. It was all in Calvin, Hiram told Larry later. Calvin promised you money and success if you stayed straight and narrow. Well, they don't come any straighter and narrower than Hiram and he had pots of money.

But when it came to *la vie intime* Hiram was on less solid ground, with his three marriages and his two troubled kids. "I never understood what went wrong with you and Ruth—except that you didn't want kids and she did."

Orbach folded his napkin into ever smaller squares. "I never understood it, either." he said. "And now I've kind of lost my nerve. Do you realize that nerve and never have exactly the same letters? I don't even know what restaurant to invite her out to."

Hiram spun out a Zagat-web of names without hesitation ending with Les Trois Canards. Orbach took notes. "I've been wondering," he said, "if I can be counted among the best or the worst?"

Hiram slid his watch out from under a starched white French cuff. "What does that mean," he asked and Orbach surprised himself by quoting the Yeats poem that the girl had tried to cheat on. *"The best lack all conviction / while the worst are full of passionate intensity."*

Hiram stood up, ready for his next counseling session, an easy shift from lives and wives to stocks and bonds. " 'Twas ever thus," he said, dropping green bills over the check like autumn leaves. "I'm afraid I'm no good at this Miles Standish stuff, no good at anything personal. Not my style. I'm sorry. You need any dough?"

"No," Orbach said, choosing not to hear the question though hard up. "But what the poem says was not always true. Not when Wordsworth recalled being young during the French Revolution. *To be alive in that dawn was bliss / and to be young was very heaven.'* "

Hiram shook his head. "God, you've really become an academic. Mom always wanted you to be a teacher."

Orbach gave him a grin. "But then Dad died and we all had to shape up."

Hiram turned back from the door. "Listen, just call Ruth, take her out to dinner and tell her what you want to say. As simple as that. You don't have to be the best *or* the worst, just who you are. How *do* you feel about having kids these days?"

Orbach took a pause for thought. It was not a glib question, it deserved a straight answer.

"Different," he said. "Much different."

On the way back to Jarman's apartment Orbach picked up a copy of the *New York Comment,* the weekly gossip newspaper printed on the funny orange-colored paper. Sonny Sondheim had a column written just for him. ". . . New York marriages seem to have a shelf-life of a year-and-a-half these days. . . . But there are ways of getting back together. Here's a simple formula. Just take whatever your positions were when you broke up and turn them upside down . . . forget about beliefs and ideas. Just go into reverse and see where you get. . . ."

Having read this, Orbach opened a living room window and leaned out gulping air and remembrance. He and Ruth, too young to do anything but love and hate; they loved Shostakovich and the Mamas and the Papas, hated the war, hated Nixon. Like Jeffrey Jarman no idea seemed to cancel out any other, you did it all at once. The worst had been full of passionate intensity—but so had the best. *To be alive in that dawn was bliss / and to be young was very heaven.*

TWO DAYS LATER HE was astonished to run into Ruth at a party given by Sonny Sondheim, a fund-raiser for Peace in the Middle East. Orbach assumed that everyone not attending was for *war* in the Middle East. Then he made the mistake of saying this to Sonny. She was not amused, looked at him oddly. "That's not funny, Larry. Maybe you've been in Washington too long?" she said.

"I've been teaching," Orbach said. "Put it down to donnish humor."

"By the way, there's Ruth," Sonny said. "Is that going to be a problem?"

The answer, of course, was yes—but the problem was delayed by one of those eruptions of discussion and laughter that he missed outside of New York. Someone had proposed the idea that the end of Communism had left us in the jungle of Capitalism with nothing to believe in except personal advantage.

George Barker, who'd grown rich building senior citizen residences, answered: "Bullshit! Communism ended up built on personal advantage—they just lied about it."

"We have safety nets."

"Full of holes," Jack Shapiro, the oldest psychoanalyst in New York, piped in. "You see any black faces here? Any poor faces?"

"What are poor faces? That's Nazi imagery." This was Jean Pflaum, who did PR for every losing Democratic candidate in memory.

"Any face you'd never see in a Woody Allen movie."

A laugh defused the air and Ruth was suddenly at Orbach's side. "Hello," he said. "I thought this was supposed to be about peace in the Middle East."

"This *is* the Middle East and we've never had peace," Ruth said, still lithe in a black sheath, still quick, clever. They moved their drinks to the terrace as if they'd had the rendezvous from the start. But it felt precipitous to Orbach; he'd wanted an encounter but a prepared one. Ruth may have felt the same way. She manufactured conversation.

"Have you made any friends in Washington?"

He told her about Jeffrey Jarman and his serial monogamy of ideas, of history as fiction.

Ruth said, jumping right in, "Reminds me of you and jobs. Each one as good as the next—each one going—"

She stopped, Orbach assumed, because anger was too close to the next words. He supplied one.

"Nowhere?"

He focused on her face, not her eyes, eyes were dangerous, eyes were meaning, ready for accusations, sensual memories, all bad paths. No, he stayed on the smooth velvet of her white, lightly fuzzed cheek. Something was wrong, something missing. Of course: the beauty mark, what he'd always called her Madame Dubarry, a tiny mole, actually. It was gone, no shadow-memory left, just a clear sweep of clean pale skin. Orbach was devastated; foolish or not, it was as if he'd lost something precious. He was a teacher now, he knew about metonymy, a part standing for a whole. The tiny Dubarry was a stand-in for Ruth. With that gone was she truly lost to him now?

Now she was responding to his provocation—the nowhere-word; she rolled out the past, not the young, bright past he'd evoked for himself and his brother, not bliss in that dawn, but his keeping life as an open question, no place for children until that question was answered, so Ruth had supplied an answer of her own, the affair, the pregnancy, the terror of the abortion and her leaving, a note on her pillow like a late-night TV movie—as if she could show him what life is truly like as an open question.

But all Orbach could say was, "What happened?"

"What do you mean?"

"To the—" He touched her cheek.

"Oh. My dermatologist took it off. She thought it might be precancerous."

But his hand touching her cheek, touching anywhere, after two years was medicine against all that old, sick stuff. He would follow the touch with a kiss, she would respond, cautiously at first, but then with the old passion; they would leave together, go to bed, they'd always been good at that, good times and bad—they'd talk about having a child, perhaps start one this very night.

And as if, indeed, they were completely alone without a fund-raising cocktail party going on a few feet behind a glass door, he kissed her. She suffered it. That's the only way to describe it. Clearly her desire had cooled. That thing they'd always had had not survived the two-year separation. Later, when he told Sonny Sondheim what had happened, what had almost happened, she said, "Listen, two years in New York is a decade, a generation."

But at the moment, the awful moment he'd been too dumb, too wound up in himself to envision, what Ruth said was, "I think not. We've done each other."

All he could think of, now, was not to let it turn sour and foolish. With a faux lightness he said, "Then how about dinner. I hear Aux Trois Poulets is good."

"God no," Ruth said. "They've gone downhill for two years." She looked at him slyly, the way you look at someone you've known long ago and are not quite sure of anymore. "Well," she said, "has it been two years?"

"Two years and three months."

"But who's counting," she said.

When they went back inside, the party had turned grimly serious. Martha Graves had arrived and she and Sonny Sondheim were facing off. Dazed with his own astonishment at finding and losing Ruth again so unexpectedly, the sour taste of disappointment in his mouth, Orbach could hardly follow the argument: West Bank, Golan Heights, security, justice for Palestinians, terrorism . . .

"How long can you live without a future?" Sonny Sondheim said, speaking for the Palestinians.

"How long can you keep living in fear?" Martha Graves said, speaking for Israel.

Others chimed in on both sides, on new sides as yet unspoken for.

Orbach edged towards the door. The best *and* the worst, he thought, each full of passionate intensity. The trouble was, he had no idea who was which.

As HE TURNED THE key in Jeffrey Jarman's lock he heard the phone ringing. By some ancient reflex Orbach raced to answer it. He did not pause to think that it was probably not for him, someone wanting Jarman, a friend, a student, a lover. But it was Geneva Brask, the Czech girl, full of apologies for disturbing him.

"It is very late."

"Are you in Washington?" Orbach had no idea why he asked such a pointless question. What did it matter where she was?

"No, I am in New York."

Orbach paused, as much to catch his breath as to give her a

chance to tell him why she was on the phone after giving him such a bad time, after cheating, after spoiling the delicate balance of his escape into the Academy.

"I want to—for you to know that I love that poem . . ." Now she paused. "The one by W. B. Yeats."

"Yes," he said. "I know which poem you mean."

"Can I come and talk to you?"

"Why?"

"I need to come and talk to you, Professor Orbach." I'm not really a professor, he thought, and this is one needy young girl; first she *needs* answers, now she *needs* to talk.

THE IDEA OF HER had been so connected to irritation, to anger at what she'd done, that Orbach had forgotten how oddly pretty she was—high Slav cheekbones, austere, her dark eyes blinking at him out of some Eastern European dream. She gave the impression of shyness but the way her body moved, small-framed, lean, direct, said the opposite. She wore a little hat actually sporting a feather, an anachronism of space if not of time; perhaps all Czech girls wore hats. Like all students she carried a book, which she placed on the small table in the foyer, like a calling card from more naïve times.

They sat on Jarman's cream-colored couch—Orbach could have used a drink but it would be rude to drink alone and he was nervous about offering a student alcohol. When she began to cry he was not prepared; Ruth had never cried and he'd kept himself deep-frozen since the breakup, had not been exposed to tears.

"What is it?" Orbach said, though he knew and knew that she knew that he knew. It was why she was here; the student/teacher crisis.

"My father," she said, surprising him. "My father is ashamed that I needed the answers so hard that I sneaked with that blue book."

In some desperation, Orbach suggested a drink.

"A vodka, ice?" Geneva Brask said.

He expected to find vodka labeled Gin and gin labeled Whiskey but Jarman's blurring of categories did not extend that far. Drink in hand, finding some resource of dignity and calm he didn't think he was in touch with anymore, especially after tonight's painful encounter with Ruth, Orbach went to Jarman's bookshelves and retrieved the *Collected Poems of Yeats*. "Look," he said. "There are no answers, only questions. A statement in a poem is not really a statement, it's a testing of waters." He was lecturing on automatic pilot out of nervousness. Wasn't he putting himself in this girl's hands just by having her up in his apartment? He was at least twenty years older and she had been a loose cannon before, could be again.

He thought: if he got in trouble with this girl, who could he call on in New York? When you yo-yoed too much the waters tended to close around you. He ran the Rolodex of memory. Jerry Sachs, if he was still in town after all his threats about quitting law and going to live with his second wife in LA; Hillary Morris, who ran the travel agency in Soho; Jan Cross, who was really more Ruth's friend; any of them would be glad to help if— if what? If a student called the police and said the Professor was sexually harassing her? Foolishness. Still, it made him feel better just to run the names in his head, less vulnerable.

He wasn't about to do a close reading of a Yeats poem late at night in a borrowed apartment with a troubled student. All he wanted to do was toss certain phrases at her. "Look," Orbach said, "'. . . the ceremony of innocence is drowned; the best lack all conviction, while the worst are full of passionate intensity . . .' Yeats wrote this in 1919, one year after the 'blood-dimmed tide' of the First World War ended. After such an awful experience, how could he not think about a different kind of second coming—not the glorious return of Jesus and the kingdom of heaven on earth but some monstrous parody: some 'rough beast slouching towards Bethlehem to be born.' You could say Yeats was visionary—after all, Fascism, Nazism, was on its way."

Those Eastern European eyes were wider than ever now, below them an eager smile. She took a deep swallow of vodka and said, "Yes," she said. "An answer."

"No, Miss Brask," he said, "an interpretation. One of a thousand." An appropriate remark for one sitting on Jeffrey Jarman's couch. "Anyway, I think you'd better go."

"But what will happen now? About the trouble?" She actually took his hand in hers. Her nail polish was some weird kind of purple. The moment her hands touched his he smelled her perfume, light, tickling his nose. Orbach sat with his hands imprisoned by Geneva Brask. It was as if she was trying to calm him instead of the other way around. After a while he said, "How did you get this phone number?"

Instead of answering she leaned forward and kissed him. Orbach hadn't kissed a woman since the breakup with Ruth. Whenever he met a woman he found interesting he would end up telling her about his wife, about his awful sense of loss, not the greatest aphrodisiac in the world. There was an instant when he could have yielded—could have made love on this couch in neutral territory, in an apartment in which history was labeled Fiction and fiction, History.

"So I was too foolish to want answers." She looked ready to weep. Her head nodded like a mechanical doll saying yes over and over. "When I am a child everybody in Prague has answers—answers for everybody else maybe not for themselves. Communism, Socialism, Dissenters, Counterrevolution. Nobody has what you call convictions but everybody has answers." Still pressing his hand between hers she said, "Thank you."

Why was she thanking him? Orbach was swept with gratitude at being with someone as adrift in questions as he was. He began to tell her about the fund-raising party, actually told her how he'd tried to kiss Ruth and how she'd declined the gambit, all of it ending in the endless fights over a distant politics no one could control. He could see quickly how foolish this was. If he didn't have the guts to accept Geneva's pass he shouldn't whine about his wife's declining *his* pass.

"The best lack all conviction while the worst . . . ," he began and then he was bending down and sealing his fate or at the very least returning a kiss that had been offered: a bribe or impulse, he had no idea and did not care.

Afterwards he found himself telling Geneva about the disappearance of his wife's beauty mark, the vanished Dubarry.

"Dubarry?" Geneva Brask murmured. Another new word in a strange language. Did she think this was a metaphor, something she could be asked on a test and pass or fail?

They lay in a welter of disarranged clothing. Orbach was concerned about the state of Jarman's couch but was too embarrassed to start examining it for stains of lovemaking, now. Also, a small panic was eating at him. "He got me drunk with vodka then he made me make love to him," she could tell the authorities. He had been in her arms, between her legs, and now he was truly in her hands.

As it turned out Jeffrey Jarman had given her the phone number. He accepted this information without pressing for the circumstances, the possible reasons. Had Geneva Brask also slept with Jarman? Had he sent her to him for occult reasons of his own? Was Jeffrey Jarman Orbach's teacher in some unnamed course everyone must take sooner or later? Orbach was determined to pass.

● ● ●

THERE WAS AN AWKWARD moment at the door. Her clothing rearranged into respectable order, she said, instead of good-bye, "You are a kind man?" It had the upward, unfinished inflection of a question. Or it could simply be that uncertain way Europeans use a language not their own, the way a Southern lawyer he knew made every statement sound unfinished. It was probably her hope that, now that they'd been intimate, surely he would drop the complaint, the proceedings, the charges. Give her an honest B for the course.

After she was gone he found she'd forgotten her book. It was a foreign paperback, published in Prague, but in English: *How Americans Make Love.* Had she been doing her homework before she arrived, brought another text into the classroom, this time the bedroom—well, anyway the living room couch? She'd also left a handkerchief on the couch where they'd made love, lace-embroidered, lightly perfumed, something from another country, an earlier century.

He pressed the handkerchief between the pages of the book, took it into the bedroom and found a place for it with the fiction, which, of course, was under the rubric History.

Something he'd missed before caught his eye. Two other categories.

Poetry: Autobiography

Autobiography: Poetry

Apparently when you began shifting categories there was no end to it, Orbach thought and prepared to sleep in Jarman's bed. He'd slept with a student. She could bring sexual harassment charges, he could drop the cheating charges. They were, in some odd way, even.

IT IS NIGHT AND Orbach is falling asleep in the New York to which he'd returned in order to hear the truth from the mouths of babes. Orbach replayed the recording of himself, in amazement, talking about Ruth to this young girl, this student; heard himself calling her my "then-wife." The girl had said, "Ruth, I like it. Sounds like truth. My mother named me after the peace treaty: Geneva."

It is night in New York and Orbach is preparing himself for sleep in Jarman's bed, preparing to stop foolishly mourning Ruth, if he can learn how to do that, if that was something that could be learned, preparing to go back to Washington, the city where the best lack all conviction, where everyone knows the Second Coming has come and gone.

Thinking of this extraordinary day, of Geneva Brask's book *How Americans Make Love,* now filed under History, Orbach's mood lightens as he drowses towards sleep. He laughs and thinks, Jarman has the right idea.

Then the phone rings and Orbach stops laughing. After a while he starts to count the rings.

One Day's Perfect Weather

Inspired by "Happiness Makes Up in Height for What It Lacks in Length,"
a poem by Robert Frost

Blazing May sunshine, but only through windows; floor-to-ceiling windows with the world well seen, but still windows between them and the sun.

"How can we both live in this bed?" Volya asks. "What a crazy idea."

"Only one of us is going to what you would call live in this bed."

"None of your gallows humor," she says. "It hurts when I laugh. But you can see how difficult it's going to be."

"You can get out of bed when you want to. Go out into the world, flirt with men in the sunny streets."

"I can't go anywhere, yet, so you shouldn't tease me. Weeks, he said, maybe months."

"That's what mine told me, too. It's mostly a matter of how many weeks or months. In some matters, quantity is everything."

The electronic timer on the endtable rings its *brrrrrrr.* Mickey reaches over and shuts it off.

"And there's going to be that sound all the time."

"Gargrrrlll."

"What?"

Mickey finishes swallowing his pills with the last splat of water in the glass. Spread all around them on the bed is the debris of a board game: dice, cards, the delicately balanced board.

"I said you should try not to be so sensitive to sounds."

She turns towards him very carefully. Her elegant legs with their muscular curves of calves are significantly longer than his. With a touch of scorn she says, "I am a dancer. Was. I am trained to respond to sound."

"You mean music, not sound."

"Hegel says music is the Ur sound, buried already in ordinary squeaks and rings of life."

"If I didn't know that you were such an extraordinary lay you would sound like a stuffed intellectual."

"You have a vulgar streak I didn't see before. Anyway, a person could be both, no? But I am not."

"They gave you Hegel at that school in Moscow?"

"They didn't give. I found. And don't patronize my youth. Or Russia. They're the same thing. What's it like out today?"

He closes his eyes and imagines the pools of sunshine on Sixth Avenue, the bicycles chained to parking meters, the sun dazzling the eyes of the pedigreed dogs in the window of the pet shop on the northeast corner.

"Sunny and warm," he tells her. "The tourists from the upper West Side and Montclair, New Jersey, will be strolling on West Tenth Street."

"More patronizing. You just envy them because they're out and you're in." Volya smiles, a touch of malice. It is radiance when that superb rictus takes her unawares. You could light up Times Square at night with that smile.

"Don't *you?*" he says. "Wouldn't it be wonderful to get out of this bed, dress up, *sportif,* and take the air in a tobacco trance."

"No quotes," she says. "Michael, you promised."

"How about your Hegel?"

"That was my life, autobiography, not quoting. We have to tell each other—*things*. I counted up last night, it's only been twelve weeks, married for four. We've hardly met."

It is Mickey's turn to smile. "That's right." He turns towards her side of the bed, grazes his hand over her small peaked breasts. "Tell me," Mickey says. "Do you come here often?"

WHILE MICKEY IS SHAVING—no matter how weak he feels he still insists on shaving every day, standing up, holding onto the bathroom sink—Bobby comes in to clear away the breakfast dishes.

"Bobby," Volya asks, "why is Michael so sharp to me, so difficult these days? He was never that way before."

"You haven't had much of a before. But maybe it's because you're both trapped in that bed. Except that yours is a temporary trap called arthritis, a virus, whatever; his is a deep, dark trap called cancer. You'll be out of that bed in weeks, months at the worst. He's not getting out. That could make a person a little edgy."

"Yes," she says.

Bobby hesitates in the doorway, juggling the breakfast trays. "You knew it when you married him, right?"

"I guess so," she says. "Still . . ."

Bobby says, "You mean there's knowing and there's knowing?"

She half-opens a smile; very low voltage.

IT WAS NEVER SUPPOSED to come to this. It was never supposed to come to anything. They'd met in a welter of metal braces, rubber tubing, She'd come forward to meet him with some sort of electronic device in her hand ready to make him strong again, ready to undo the harm the "problem" had already done, to his bones, his joints, his ligaments. He never called it anything but the "problem." It was his way of reducing it to manageable proportions. The thing itself was all-powerful, in charge of life and death. But a "problem" was something you dealt with, a "problem" was something you might solve.

Stretching him on the rack, forcing him to pull more weight than he could have pulled before, she told him how dangerous that way of thinking was.

"Pull," she said softly. "Harder, but slowly. The slower you do your exercises the better they build the strength."

Wheezing but playful with her, he asked, "Do you think I'll still be able to make the beast with two backs?"

"Pulllll," she intoned. "That is a quote. Shakespeare. Don't make conversation with quotes. Make your own."

"I mean—considering my 'problem' . . ."

"Where I come from when you call something what it's not, everybody lives a lie. It's disgusting!"

"Moscow?"

"Leningrad. Now St. Petersburg."

"*Now?*" He tried to make her smile. He could always seduce his actresses, his actors, his designers, everybody.

She obliged and the smile blew him away. Day and night were included in that face, dark and subtle in repose, brilliant under the stretch of one of her many different smiles. She was an unexpected side effect of treatment.

"It's called St. Petersburg—now and then," she said. "Every fifty years or so. You can rest for one hundred and twenty seconds."

"You mean two minutes."

"You are not directing this production. I said one hundred and twenty seconds. You can wipe your sweat with this."

She slung a towel over his shoulder and walked away on astonishing legs.

NOW, SHE ASKS, A challenge: "What would you do, exactly, if we could keep on making what you so charmingly call 'the beast with two backs'? What that's fresh and new?"

"Ha," he rises to the bait. "None of your old world we've-seen-it-all cynicism! I can think of a thousand positions with no echoes of lovers from life or literature."

She leans carefully but elegantly on a slender forearm. "Start with one," she says.

Mickey has been challenged before—hundreds of actresses calling down from the stage into the darkness of the orchestra, asking for a precise example to back up an instruction or interpretation. He doesn't take a beat. "I would make love to you in a car—"

"Ha! Big deal! Every teenager in the world—"

"—In a car, in the front seat, during an automatic car wash—the great golem of the machine-brushes whipping across the windows and windshield while we—"

"Michael, that's not a *position*."

"No, but it would be thrilling, it would be extraordinary."

"Okay, it would be unusual. But positions!"

Now Mickey allows himself a little thinking time. In a formal, announcing voice, he says: "The Porcupine Position."

"The what?"

"No *interruptus* please. In this position the man and woman circle each other very carefully, touching each other only on the smooth insides of surfaces; they never lose control even at the end."

Volya was laughing. Her laughter did not move Mickey the

way her smiles did. It was healthy laughter but not luminous. "Then how do they ever get to the end?"

"The usual way—or ways. And if it's successful, no skin is pierced. You've heard of blood lust. This position is bloodless lust."

Brrrr. The bedside timer rang its bloodless reminder: medicine time. Pills swallowed, invention resumed.

"Okay," he says. "The Rodeo Position."

"The *what?*"

"Rodeo. In this position, the woman tries to run out of the bedroom, the man lassos her with a lariat—"

"What is lary-at?"

"It's a rope with a loop tied in it to catch a steer or a calf usually. But this is an adaptation for sexual purposes."

Her clear blue eyes open wide. "I am to be steer or calf?"

"You don't care for that position? Then how about this one: the Professor Position. In this position the woman lies in bed naked, reading a book, preferably literary criticism. The man lies next to her, also naked, and caresses her, then makes love, complete passionate love to her; she continues reading until they are both finished. Afterwards, he smokes a cigarette and gives her a spot quiz about the book she was reading."

"You're crazy." But she gets the idea and turns on a three-hundred-watt grin.

THE LATE MORNING TURNS bad. Volya cannot find a place to lie without hurting. She's afraid to stand. She phones the doctor and gets his service who asks her if it's an emergency. She says no it's not an emergency, changes her mind, yes, it's a terrible emergency, hangs up and tries not to breathe. If the entire universe is still, perhaps she will feel no pain. Also, it has come and gone swiftly in the past, so it is always accompanied by hope.

"Michael," she says. "Let's trade."

"What?"

"I'll take your 'problem.' You take mine."

He pretends to think carefully about her offer. "I don't know," he says. "I wouldn't mind the extra years—but I don't take pain too well."

"Yes, but you would have years to learn."

"True."

SHE (extending her hand): Deal?

HE (shaking her hand): Deal!

SHE: Will you miss me?

HE: Like crazy! In between spasms of pain, mind you.

SHE: I miss you, already.

HE: Not fair. I'm still here. Remember in Camus' play Caligula at the end being stabbed by the members of his court, shouting in between the knife thrusts: "I'm still here." I did a production in St. Paul, Minnesota, one February. Snowed in. Only one person in the audience—a man who doesn't take off his coat or snowy hat all during the performance. Kenneth Haig playing Caligula. When Ken is being stabbed and calls out "I'm still here," the guy stands up and says, "Well, I'm not," and exits.

Volya looks at him coolly.

"This really happened?"

"Well, no, actually. It was a company joke. You have to do something when you're snowed in with twenty actors in St. Paul. God, how will I ever learn what makes a Russian woman laugh?"

To make up for his deception he caresses her, promisingly, a gliding hand closer to pay dirt than he's come in days, uncertain as he is that his "problem" will allow him to deliver on any promise. She lays her head on his shoulder, eyes half-closed, breathing through her mouth. But the doctor returns her emergency call at that moment and advises an increase in the Percodan. Then Bobby comes in with lunch. Just to drive him crazy Mickey tells him about the trade deal. He looks at them with despair.

"When are you guys going to grow up?" he says.

Bobby is twenty-four, black, or rather dusty brown, but already very grown up; Caucasian features, a Jamaican mother and a Jewish father, he pointed out to Mickey when applying for the job as his assistant. He could convincingly play any role, white, black, green, he'd said, not limited to traditional casting. He wanted to work closely with a director like Mickey Stamos—and there was no director like Mickey, only the man himself, the man who created mad, ambitious projects, the man who revived Sartre's *Kean,* who mounted a twelve-hour adaptation of *Thus Spake Zarathustra.* The man whose hallmark as a director was that he could make comedy out of anything.

Bobby got the job and Mickey was promptly confined to bed. The "problem" had arrived and Bob went from being devoted theatrical acolyte to nursemaid, script-reader, bill-payer, project researcher, prescription-filler and cook. He was happy but there would be no acting roles, traditional or otherwise, until the "problem" resolved itself. What gave him the most trouble was watching Mickey make comedy out of what was happening to him.

By the time Bobby returned to clear away the lunch trays it had turned stormy out, the sun obscured by swirling clouds, spring rain threatening.

"Bobby," Volya says, "we are newlyweds. Suppose we want to make love? I mean you bounce in and out without knocking or anything."

"I assumed that was out. I mean I thought you were in this great *douleur.* From now on I'll knock," Bobby says. He balances trays, privacies, egos. Also, he has a little French to put on display, having played Molière, having played Racine. Right now, it's Robert Frost who is his anxious concern.

He lingers.

"Yes?" Volya says, slightly imperial, as if the sex in question might commence on the instant.

But Bobby is talking to Mickey. When two people are in bed it's sometimes hard to know who's being addressed. The beast with four legs.

"I think I may have the Frost poem you need for the close of the show."

"Great," Michael half sat up in bed. "What do you think? Birches: *One could do worse than be a swinger of birches.* Or, here: *Good fences make good neighbors . . .*" Michael the actor, onstage at age six with his famous father, is onstage once more, intoning in bed, an audience of two will do.

"Well, no. I don't think one of the war-horses is a great idea. You need something fresh, something the audience doesn't know. But one that still will pack a punch."

"Ah." Mickey subsides but Volya rises. "I don't think you're doing Michael a favor by going on with the charade of a new play." (She pronounced it a la Russe, Mik-ai-el, had dismissed the nickname, early on. "Mickey, a name for a boy not for a man.") "What is the matter with both of you?"

"Charade?" Mickey may be still acting. It's difficult to know. "Do you know what I went through to get the rights from the Frost estate?"

Exasperated, Volya shifts suddenly towards Mickey. A distortion of pain crosses her face. "But you are bedridden . . . you are—"

Bobby freezes, trays in hand, trying not to look at Mickey. Volya has almost said the unsayable. But he underestimates Mickey's sangfroid in the face of the "problem."

"Anyway, lying down or standing up, I am going to produce *Frost!* But I'm still not happy with the title. *Frost!* It sounds like a Christmas musical for children, not a biographical play about a great poet. What do you think, Volya?"

She turns away, giving up on him for the moment. It was something she'd been doing a lot of since the impulsive marriage less than a month ago. Mickey was the first patient she had ever gone out with or slept with, let alone married, and Volya was convinced that she was being punished by whatever gods were in charge of professional conduct. They'd begun with Shakespeare-in-the-Park, a production of *Othello*—where Iago had spoken to them of the beast with two backs. From there they'd progressed to long dinners and longer adolescent-style groping sessions.

"You're as nervous as I am," she'd murmured against his chest one night. "It is your famous 'problem,' yes?"

Three times a week he continued to arrive at physiotherapy, to be stretched on the rack in the name of strength, in the name of restoring health. When it all began to feel too weird to her, she suggested they stop going out or that he find another physiotherapist.

Instead they fled to City Hall to be married. When her courage failed her, on the trip downtown, Mickey held her hand in a tight grasp.

"It's instant citizenship. Think of it that way," he'd said.

"Instant widow," she said, already teary.

"I'll leave exact instructions about how to invest the estate. Being a widow is a better job than being a physiotherapist."

"I like being a physiotherapist."

"Then you can do both." He had more arguments, more wit than she had strength to resist. They continued their journey to City Hall. It was the only possible end to the roller coaster ride they were on. The "problem" did not intrude itself on their honeymoon, which was a trip to Brighton Beach, Little Odessa, the signs in Cyrillic, Russian songs blaring from loudspeakers outside record stores—"It's the closest thing to meeting your family," Mickey told her. Bobby came along for the nightclub trip and left them at a hotel near the boardwalk, where all went well that night and continued well, through his first preproduction days of *Frost!*, though by then he needed a cane to help him navigate and the necessary retreat to the bed was only a few weeks away.

Nevertheless, things continued well for the next two weeks, until Volya's virus hit, collapsing her down several unseen steps to the ladies' room during a rehearsal. It turned out to be a peculiar virus which aggravates incipient arthritic conditions.

"But I have always been a healthy horse," she told the doctor. She lied, of course. It was the bone pain which had made her give up being a dancer, which had turned her, instead, to the ballet of ropes and chrome and the stretching of other people's muscles.

"Many dancers have arthritis without knowing it. They sort of hurt in their bones all the time, anyway, so they don't find out—until they have to. That's the bad news."

"I understand," Volya said, grim.

The doctor was young, smiling, lighthearted. "No, no," he said. "That's a joke. You're supposed to ask about the good news."

"I don't understand American jokes."

"The good news is, these viruses are self-limiting. Three weeks, eight weeks, two or three months. Then they go away."

She cheered up, considerably, after hearing this. "We will call it my 'problem,'" she told Mickey, needling him with confidence now that her fear was diminished.

"Don't push your luck," Mickey had said and plunged into *Frost!* with a vengeance, a stream of visitors arriving at bedside with set designs in hand, with contracts to sign, with production schedules.

"IF YOU CAST HAL Holbrook or James Whitmore as Frost I'm quitting," Bobby said.

"What's your choice?" Mickey said. "Sidney Poitier? Morgan Freeman?"

"I don't need somebody black, just somebody fresh."

Hence Foster Lanier, a young actor fresh from Yale Drama School, having spouted a stream of bona fides—a touring company of *Streetcar, Salesman* at Seattle Rep—now standing near the doorway of the enormous bedroom, and in the middle of reading, in a rich and ripe Southern accent, the poem Bobby had discovered for the opening and close of the play:

> . . . I can but wonder whence
> I get the lasting sense
> of so much warmth and light.
> If my mistrust is right
> It may be altogether
> From one day's perfect weather,
> When starting clear at dawn
> The day swept clearly on . . .

It may have been the strangest audition setting in the history of the theater. Mickey, wearing a paisley robe, propped up in bed on a mass of pillows, notebook on his lap, reading glasses dangling from a red cord around his neck, Volya next to him, listening attentively, trying not to look embarrassed, and Bobby on a folding chair near the bathroom, clipboard in hand.

When the young man finished his reading, his voice strained, his cheeks flushed red, Mickey said, softly, "Robert

Frost was Mister New England. Foster, you're from the South, aren't you?"

"Mobile," he said. "But ah can alter mah diction. Ah've done it before."

The silence in the room was deadly. Surprising everyone, herself, too, Volya broke it.

"My mother saw Robert Frost. Before I was born. In Moscow."

Quickly, Bobby stood. "We have your phone numbers," he said. "Thanks for coming to read."

"The service can always find me," the actor said and when he was gone Volya turned on the two men.

"I never would dream you had such bad character, such bad faith."

"What?" Mickey was all innocence. "What do you mean?"

"You lead people on. That boy thinks he has a chance for a part in a play that will happen."

"So?"

She ran blood into her cheeks much like the actor had. "You are making promises you have no intention of keeping."

Bobby had left the room, as soon as he saw the trouble coming. He was good at exits.

"Darling," Mickey said. "I know what you mean. But there's always a chance of a swan song. It's only a seven-week rehearsal period. I didn't know your mother saw Robert Frost."

She went from a rage to a sulk, swiftly. "He was on a tour; Khrushchev made it possible for Americans to come and everybody loves Robert Frost in Russia. My mother stood in line for four hours to get in to hear. She was very happy."

"I love learning things about you," Mickey said. "Everything's new."

She kissed him, quickly. "I am your swan song, is it not?"

"It is," he said. "And don't forget, swans mate for life."

"This," she said and smiled, "will not be too hard in our case."

He moved back to work, his old life-saving habit. "What did you think of the 'Happiness' poem? Is it the right one?"

"I liked the lines, 'O stormy, stormy world, the days you were not swirled around . . .'"

But she told him she needed to read it, slowly, to herself, and then out loud. She told him of reading poems and essays by Frost in school and at home. One essay in particular had been very important to her. Her English was not quite up to it but it was something to do with grief and grievance—she couldn't recall the name.

He tossed the fat red-covered paperback of poems and prose to her. "Read it and weep," he said. "I'm going to the bathroom." They had not yet reached the total confinement stage, what Mickey called the bedpan-humor stage, of their gallows-humor situation. He could still navigate to the bathroom and back.

Volya riffled through the pages and found sentences, bits and pieces. She was looking for two key words she remembered. As if need were magic she found them swiftly.

But for me, Frost wrote, *I don't like grievances. . . . What I like is griefs. . . . Grievances are a form of impatience. Griefs are a form of patience. . . . Grievances are something that can be remedied, and griefs are irremediable . . .*

Having held off tears and fear with equal strength, Volya was not prepared for the power of the simple word "griefs." English was not her language but she had learned it as a child, had liked its song. Now a few English words were shaking her bed-solid poise, threatening tears.

. . . there is solid satisfaction in a sadness that is not just a fishing for ministry and consolation. Give us immedicable woes—woes that nothing can be done for—woes flat and final.

Some of the words were hopeless for her to understand, but she got the sense, in all its bright and clever darkness. Mickey returned from the bathroom and caught the glistening in the corners of her eyes. He eased himself into the bed and turned to look for the words which had brought the first hint of tears he'd ever seen in Volya. Quickly she flipped the book shut.

"Can't I see?" he asked.

"No," she said. "Not yet."

THE GAME WAS CALLED Flights and Fancies, a knock-off of Dungeons and Dragons, only less mystical. When a player was trapped there were "flights" prepared for escape. But you also needed "fancies," imaginings, chosen by a throw of the dice. It was a board game and used dice and you could play it in bed, so Mickey had become a bit addicted to it. Volya could take it or leave it and Bobby was restless. He had been pressed into playing by Mickey, when he wanted to get back to work.

Mickey, normally the High Priest of Work, said, "Play is everything."

"I thought *the* play was the thing."

"Please," Mickey admonished him. "Volya does not trust men who use literary quotations in their conversation."

"Volya doesn't trust me, anyway."

"You think not?" Mickey was interested. He moved a counter and opened up an avenue for flight. "Why do you think?"

"Because I'm bad for you. I encourage your delusions."

"Like what?"

At this Bobby packed in the game. "Okay, I'll be in the office trying to get our playwright up here to discuss one of your delusions, this afternoon. Our production of his play."

"Don't make it too late," Mickey said.

"He gets tired in the afternoon," Volya told Bobby.

"Don't ever talk in front of me as if I'm not here," Mickey said, perhaps the first testy thing he'd ever said to Volya. "I'm still here."

"And you're still my Caligula," she smiled and he laughed out loud and started to kiss her. From the roiling skies beyond the window thunder cracked the air.

"Some spring," Bobby muttered as rain smashed against the bedroom windows.

"Listen to you," Volya said. "You can go where you want. If I don't get away from these walls and these sheets soon, out into the air, I'll go crazy."

Mickey climbed out of bed. "Jesus, every time I hear the rain I have to pee. Just like a child."

While he is in the bathroom, Bobby tries to enlist Volya's support for the poem he wants.

"It has this weird title."

"Which?"

"Happiness Makes Up in Height for What It Lacks in Length."

"Yes," she said. "Weird."

"It's just the poet wondering out loud about having the sense, for his whole life, of a world full of sunlight and brightness, when for so much of the time he remembers it being swirled around with clouds, stormy, dark."

"That's all?" Volya asked.

"Then he decides, maybe it's just from the memory of one perfect day, when he and his lover, his wife, his friend, I don't know which, when they walked out together for one whole day of perfect sunshine and clear skies."

Volya thought for a moment. "I don't like it when you explain poetry. I have to read it." She examined Bobby's smooth brown face, closely. "Tell me, Bobby, why is it so important that this poem is to be picked for the play?"

"Oh, God." He sat himself down on the rumpled bed. "The playwright is set on it. Mickey wanted one of the famous poems, the ones kids learn in school, and I don't want him getting all upset, getting into a fight, making himself sick." He looked across the bed at Volya. "Did your mother really see Robert Frost?" he asked.

THE PLAYWRIGHT, HAROLD HOWE, was short and round, passionate.

"You need a scene to dramatize the poem, if we're going to use it as our closing." He waved his one free hand, the other hand hefting the book of Frost poems. "Look," he said. "It's Frost at the very end, the old, white-haired prophet, the sacred icon, dying." Harold Howe read:

> O stormy, stormy world,
> The days you were not swirled
> Around with mist and cloud,
> Or wrapped as in a shroud,
> And the sun's brilliant ball
> Was not in part or all
> Obscured from mortal view—
> Were days so very few . . .

Mickey broke into the pause. "Will the audience be able to hold on to the sense of it, Harold?"

"Sure. It's just an old man looking back on a dark and stormy life—that's what the audience will register. Don't forget they'll be seeing a failing Frost, almost at the end." He ploughed ahead, a man who had spent a life convincing directors, producers, lyricists, composers.

> I can but wonder whence
> I get the lasting sense
> Of so much warmth and light.
> If my mistrust is right
> It may be altogether
> From one day's perfect weather . . .

"That, right there, that's the central wonder of it," Harold Howe was like a teacher, book in hand, two of his students in bed, and one sitting on an easy chair taking notes. "The memory of one day's perfect clear weather ransoming a whole life. To produce the effect of clarity there are three 'clears' in three consecutive lines."

> When starting clear at dawn
> The day swept clearly on
> To finish clear at eve.
> I verily believe
> My fair impression may
> Be all from that one day . . .

"Then getting out of his sickbed to walk—with only the shade of his wife, to whom he'd been so cruel, for one perfect day from sunup to sunset. Then he comes home and dies." Harold Howe closed the book. "Happiness makes up in height for what it lacks in length." He turned to face Mickey directly.

"It's a beauty," Mickey said. "I admit that, Harold. But it has archaic words like verily and whence."

Harold Howe was quick on his feet. "That just gives it the classic feel. Underlines the idea that Frost was our Wordsworth."

Mickey's eyes were closed. Bobby said, "Volya, what do you think?"

She gave him a conspirator's smile. Not one of her dazzlers; veiled. "It's beautiful," she said. She seemed to have forgotten her irritation with delusions. "The whole idea is beautiful."

"How will we show the walk?" Mickey said, eyes still closed.

"Rear projection," Harold Howe said happily.

THAT NIGHT, AS THEY prepared for sleep, Mickey complained, for the first time, about their confinement. "I'd like to be one of those tourists from New Jersey," he said, "soaking up the sunshine and buying stupid souvenirs, lamps that don't work when you get them home and T-shirts that say I LOVE NEW YORK, with a heart where the word LOVE goes. Anything just to get out, not to be trapped."

Wind joined the rain and the window across from the bed rattled in its frame.

"Yes." She shook out a Percodan into her palm and poured the necessary water. "I have the same grievance. That is the right word?"

"The perfect word."

She swallowed the pill with a quick shake of her head and opened the Frost collection. "I found it here. I think this was the essay I read in the kitchen at home, when I was a kid."

She read, *"I don't like grievances. What I like is griefs."*

He reached. "Let me see that."

She held the book away from him and kept reading. *"Grievances are a form of impatience. Grief is a form of patience."* Mickey nodded, settling back on his pillow. "Right," he murmured. "I'm damned impatient with the room inside and the rain outside."

"Give us immedicable woes—woes that nothing can be done for— woes flat and final," she read.

"Was that what you were reading yesterday that got you a little teary." It was not a question.

"Michael." Volya frowned. "What is im-medic-able?"

"Frost tells you: flat and final. Something there's no medicine for."

"Ah." She handed him the book. "But look—look what he says next."

Mickey read, *"Woes flat and final. And then to play. The play's the thing. Play's the thing . . ."*

He grinned shyly at her. "The old boy was a mind reader. There's got to be a place for this stuff in the play. I'll show it to Harold."

Volya lay back and clicked the room into darkness. "I think," she whispered, "he was playing with play—not *a* play, or *the* play. Just play."

She smoothed a lotion over those long dancer's legs and Mickey smelled walnuts.

"Are there nuts in that stuff?"

"It's called Forest Cream. Maybe."

Mickey lay listening to the wild rain for a moment, on the edge of a wonderful idea, and not just an idea—something to be done—something absolutely extraordinary, something about griefs and grievances, happiness and play, edging at his mind and even deeper, where his breath came from. But the Valium and the Percodan had both done their work and before he could grasp the idea, he joined Volya in sweet, medicated sleep.

MICKEY WAKES EARLY, MUCH earlier than usual. The digital clock gives red hours: 6:05 A.M. He is usually a slow waker. This morning he is alert at once. The vague notion of the night before is crystal clear. It is no longer an idea; it has become an action, a scheme, however crazy. The only question will be: can

Volya handle it without too much pain, and will he be strong enough.

He reaches for the long cord Bobby has placed near him. A flood of sunlight bathes the room. The storm is past and the idea of spring is back. Volya is still asleep behind her sleep mask.

"Pssst, Volya." He touches her shoulder gently. She rolls towards him—a moan of pain comes, though she still sleeps. Then she reaches up and pushes the black silk mask from her eyes, looks at him with eyes rimmed red from days of exhausting hurt.

"What, Michael, what?"

He tells her of the plan. They will leave the bed, they *will leave* the house, secretly, Bobby still asleep, all doctors far away; they *will play* in the fields of sunny streets, of green parks, walk, as carefully or carelessly as they can manage, as long as they can manage. They will forget pain, problems, grievances and griefs. They will have one day, acting out the Frost happiness poem, testing its truth.

Volya dresses very carefully, holding onto the bed as needed. She takes a slow step; no real pain, yet. Maybe a quick twinge. Mickey has gotten ready in a flash, a director eager to prove his concept can work.

Outside the six steps of the stoop wait, the first challenge. Mickey feels a surge of weakness, but leans on Volya, feels stronger, quickly, perhaps because of the excitement of the risky adventure.

IT IS A DAY that would have been thrilling even if nothing was being tested. The sun floats among bunches of clouds, the colors all pure, cloud-white, sun-yellow, undiluted, unshaded. Someone has hosed the streets down in front of the fruit market on Sixth Avenue.

Now: what to do? A poodle sleeps in the window of the fancy pet shop on the corner. Past Boccigaluppi's Funeral Parlor, past gelato stands, is the flower market where Mickey buys Volya a gardenia, which she wears in her hair, but loses in the cab uptown to Central Park.

"What day is this?" she asks. "I lose track cooped up in that bedroom."

"Sunday," he says. "Central Park will be lively."

In the park the last few clouds vanish and the sun dominates the sky and the day; yet it is cool enough to walk comfortably.

A park bench is a danger. If they sat down would they have the strength to get up again? They walk on, feeling strong, feeling triumphant. Later, they feel safe enough to rest on a bench, Volya's head on his arm, as if they were on a date, or newlyweds, something as banal as that. At noon when the sun becomes a touch too relentless they try to stand in the shadow of a slender tree, but it gives little shade in that perfect sunshine, so they walk on. A child, the one they would probably never have, throws a ball at them and Volya actually bends, supple and swift, to pick it up and throw it back. She looks at Mickey, startled at herself and her luck: no pain. The Percodan rests safely in her purse, slung over her shoulder.

Once, concerned, Mickey suggests she take one, as prevention for pain. No, she does not want to dull the day; she'll gamble. But passing a public phone booth she grows concerned, they must call Bobby.

Bobby: My God, where are you? Are you all right?

Mickey: We're just out for a walk.

Bobby: A walk. But how about Volya—and you're not strong enough. Come back, now, for God's sake.

Mickey: See you later.

There is a band concert in the park, but at first the sunny joy they've taken for their own is beyond sound; it's as if the band's music is muffled and simply seeing the players move their hands and mouths in playing their instruments, a silent movie, gives Mickey and Volya pleasure.

For an instant Mickey feels the old weakness topple his balance, even though he is sitting on the grass. His head goes around or the sky, it's not clear which. But he sits up slowly and the sagging weakness is gone.

As they walk on, all of a sudden the sound of the music sweeps over them, something wonderfully silly by Von Suppe, the drumbeat and the harmonies of the oboes and clarinets bring tears of happiness to Volya's eyes. She feels foolish.

LUNCH WAS A HOT dog and a Coke from a wagon near the lake, where couples escaped from a Monet past, from a Seurat dream, rowed the waters. Afternoon tea was weak, lukewarm liquid in cardboard containers at the zoo, some animal in the distance screaming pain or pleasure, hunger or boredom, the perfect sun lower in the sky, shadows now more available but less necessary.

Giddy with freedom but afraid that the day was shutting down around them, amid the cardboard containers and the crumbs of cake, they broke up the poem and fed it to each other, like children reading a favorite story over and over again, turning a meditation into the prose of passionate conversation:

"I can but wonder whence I get the lasting sense of so much warmth and light . . ."

Volya replied, as if answering his question:

"It may be altogether from one day's perfect weather. . . . My fair impression may be all from that one day . . ."

Mickey's voice trembled with fatigue. He scraped his chair along the stone closer to hers and leaned his head on her shoulder.

"*. . . No shadow crossed but ours as through its blazing flowers we went from house to wood for change of solitude.*"

They knew better than to talk much, knew better than to discuss anything. It was enough to steal the words from Frost. And Mickey knew better than to wear any of his ironic masks. It occurred to him that it had been a day without irony, a day sprinkled with laughter but without jokes. There had been none of the sharp-edged byplay, the verbal fencing, which had been the currency of their courtship. They were happy. It was enough.

"What a day," Volya muttered. There was now a throbbing pain in her right leg and in the small of her back. But she registered it as from a distance, the way the music had played behind a shield of sunlight. She did not mention the pain.

"Yes." Mickey sighed.

THE SIGHT OF THE prison-bedroom was as thrilling as the first sight of the open streets had been. Bobby helped them off with their clothes, alternately angry, or sulking, alternately frightened and relieved. He wanted to call the doctor, either doctor.

"No," Mickey said. "It's the most perfect Sunday afternoon since the beginning of the world. Let the doctors picnic with their families."

"Let them play golf," Volya giggled. Surreptitiously, she reached for the vial of Percodan.

"We have something important to tell you, Bobby." Mickey sounded a little drunk, exhaustion reaching his voice.

"Yes," Volya said.

"I'll be pleased to hear it once you're both back in bed."

They chanted it at him, one after the other. Mickey began.

"Happiness . . ."

" . . . Makes up . . ." Volya sang out.

" . . . In height . . . "

" . . . What it lacks . . . "

" . . . For length . . ." Mickey was short of breath and laughing now at the same time.

"No—*for* what it lacks *in* length." Volya corrected him, pleased at a small success in English.

They collapsed on the bed laughing, Mickey desperately weak again, Volya trembling with pain, as Bobby performed his own chant above them: about anxiety, about calls to 911, about responsibility to others.

HAPPY AND EXHAUSTED, THEY were too hopped up for sleep.

"I feel like I do after an opening," Mickey told her. "Tired but wired."

"And I feel like when I passed an audition," Volya said. "Ready for more."

Silly with fatigue, Mickey made up a new game for them to play, a board game with no need of a board, using the words she'd read to him. Instead of Dungeons and Dragons, instead of Flights and Fancies, it would be Grievances and Griefs.

"How do we play it?"

"The name tells you—you tell me a grievance and I match it with a grief. Then I do a grievance and you do a grief."

"How do we know the difference?"

"You told it to me from Frost. Grievances are impatient. Griefs are patient."

Volya spread lotion on her hands and arms; a walnut smell arrived in the air. She reached back and found a grievance, never a long reach.

"My mother wanted me to dance because my cousin Mira danced—and Mira was the daughter she really wanted."

"Pretty good," Mickey said. "Okay—a grief." Pause. "Griefs

are harder." A longer pause. "My mother died when she was forty-three; a sad, funny woman. She never saw a play I directed."

"Poor lady," Volya said quietly.

"She was proud of me anyway. Now I do a grievance. My first wife, Anna, the one I never talk about, she was always too busy to think about having a child. And by the time she slowed down enough, I didn't want it to be *her* child."

"No fair," Volya said. "That's a grief. Because now you have no children."

"How do we know?" Mickey threw a laugh. "You could be pregnant right now. But you're right. I wasted a good one." A beat. "Here's one—my father never thought what I did was worth a damn until the first hit I had. A crummy musical, but money talked. Now you."

This reach was harder for Volya, slower. "I left my home because life was so hard there, and my brother Mikhail—"

"I didn't know your brother had the same name as me."

"—He was doing drugs and drinking so I took him with me to America but he ran back home and left me alone in Brighton Beach."

"My God."

She produced a smile. *"Voilà,"* she said. "A grief."

"A grievance," he announced. "I don't have a real audience, a real public. They know Eisenstein, Chaplin, Reinhardt, they know Coppola, Scorcese. Nobody knows who I am except other directors."

"I married a man because I was confused and attracted and stupid in love and now he's leaving me."

"But I'm still here," Mickey said. "Anyway, which category is that?"

"Ha. You don't know your ass from a grief."

"I think maybe I do," he said. He waited and when he spoke he placed each word with slow care. "I thought there would be more time," he said. "I've been checking my watch every few minutes since I was a kid. But I always assumed there would be enough time. Dumb!"

She was tempted to pack the game in, then. But she took a breath and took her turn. "I mostly know dancers and so many are gay I'll probably never get married again."

His turn: "If dying is like lying down when you're as tired as I am maybe it won't be so bad."

Her turn: "Are you really saying truth about the famous 'problem'? And not even a complaint."

"A friend of mine says, never speak in euphemisms. It's to live a lie and it's what led to the fall of Communism. Anyway, I think I'm finished playing."

But Volya wasn't through. Forgetting that it was only a game, she barreled on into the disappointing past. She was to have danced *Swan Lake* at the Leningrad Ballet Academy graduation—but old Kasakov, her teacher, he of the herring breath and the wandering hands, was sleeping with Sonia, another dancer whose mother didn't watch her as closely as Volya's mother watched *her* daughter. Kasakov gave Sonia the part of the Dying Swan and broke Volya's teenaged heart.

She threw off the covers and raised two long, perfect legs, scissoring them open and shut and said, with passion, her voice roughening, losing control, "My body promised me a career, a life as a dancer, and then betrayed me."

He reached for her and hoped she wasn't crying, that his foolish game hadn't broken her down. "Oh, Mickey," she said. It was the first time she'd used his nickname but he sure as hell was not going to call her attention to it.

"Come here," he said, snaking her along the sheets, her legs V-ing towards him. "Your body promised me a few things, too. You still owe me some, more than I'm ever going to have time to collect."

"You can't owe bodies," she said, serious. "But you can offer them."

"I accept," he said into her open lips, then opening thighs, mouths, everything, legs, hands and even eyes all moist, wide open, unprotected, generous.

"Mickey," she whispered, "who won the game?"

"It's a tie," Mickey said. "That particular game is always a tie."

Afterwards, they lay long in the gathering darkness talking, remembering, until they could no longer see each other but could only hear each other's voice; husband and wife acquainted at last, telling their lives, swapping griefs and grievances until the grievances were gone and only grief was left and finally even grief was still.

Gloria Stern

DANIEL STERN is the Cullen Distinguished Professor of English in the Creative Writing Program at the University of Houston. He is the author of nine novels, three books of short stories, a play, and several screenplays. His novel *Who Shall Live, Who Shall Die* won the International Prix du Souvenir awarded by Elie Wiesel. In 1990 he won the American Academy of Arts and Letters Rosenthal Award for literary distinction for his book of short stories *Twice Told Tales*. he has won the *Paris Review*'s John Train Humor Award and several O'Henry Prizes for the short story, and his work has also appeared in *Best American Short Stories* and the *Pushcart Prize Anthology*. The Texas Institute of Letters awarded him the Brazos Prize for the best short story of 1996. His stories have been dramatized on National Public Radio and public television. In 1992 his adaptation of Ibsen's Hedda Gabler was produced by the American Repertory Theater in Cambridge. He has also been a cellist with Charley Parker's band and the Indianapolis Symphony Orchestra as well as a senior executive at Warner Bros., CBS television, and McCann-Erickson advertising. Professor Stern has taught at Wesleyan University, New York University, and Harvard University and has lectured at the Sorbonne.